T0003157

a respectable woman

a respectable woman

EASTERINE KIRE

zubaan

ZUBAAN
128 B Shahpur Jat,
1st floor
New Delhi 110 049
Email: contact@zubaanbooks.com
Website: www.zubaanbooks.com

First published by Zubaan Publishers Pvt. Ltd 2019

Copyright © Easterine Kire, 2019

All rights reserved

10 9 8 7 6 5 4 3 2 1

ISBN 978 93 85932 47 2

Zubaan is an independent feminist publishing house based in New Delhi with a strong academic and general list. It was set up as an imprint of India's first feminist publishing house, Kali for Women, and carries forward Kali's tradition of publishing world quality books to high editorial and production standards. *Zubaan* means tongue, voice, language, speech in Hindustani. Zubaan publishes in the areas of the humanities, social sciences, as well as in fiction, general non-fiction, and books for children and young adults under its Young Zubaan imprint.

Typeset in Baskerville 11/13 by Jojy Philip, New Delhi 110 015
Printed and bound at Thomson Press, Faridabad, India

For JJ and all the women in my life

❀

Acknowledgements

I thank my interviewees who were so gracious with their time and knowledge. They shared their memories of Kohima with me and helped me visualise the post-war years. This book came into being largely because of your help in sharing with me oral information of our history and culture and stories, and in particular, historical details of Kohima in its growing years.

Thank you, Uncle Lanu Toy, Charles Chasie, T. Solo, Pastor Sehu Belho, Visakhonu Hibo, Metsiü Iralu, Mene Kevichüsa, my mother Khrienguü Kire, Neilaü (Marion) Sircar, Adiü (Lily) Das, Aziebu Shaiza, Vitsomeno Shaiza, Kruzolie Solo, Teiso Tungoe, Atuo Mezhür, Ziebou Kire, David Kire, Agu Joanne Kire, Alen Sekhose, Raj Thapa, Seluokieü Shüya.

Thank you Jelle JP Wouters, for invaluable help with documents and additional information.

Last but not least, a big thank you to Manipal University (MCPH) and its 'writer-in-residence' programme where I spent productive weeks in January and *A Respectable Woman* began to take shape. And an equally big thank you to Artica Svalbard for hosting me at the 'Artist-in-Residence' programme where I could work further on the novel.

Zubaan, thank you for believing in the book!

Part One

ONE

After the War

It took my mother, Khonuo, exactly forty-five years before she could bring herself to talk about the war. She was ten years old when the Japanese invaded our hills in 1944. Their family was part of the mass evacuation of people from Kohima village to the villages of Chieswema, Meriema, Rüsoma, and Jotsoma. They spent more than two months sheltering in Rüsoma, which was considered a safer place than Kohima. In 1979, when I turned eighteen, my relationship with my mother smoothened out. I think it was because I had come past the tumultuous years of adolescence and rebellion and had settled into a course of study that I really liked. I enrolled to take a Bachelor's degree in English Literature and eagerly dove into the course work and intensive reading that it involved.

Azuo, as we called our mother, had spent a third of her life as a teacher of History. One day, as I was struggling with an assignment on Shakespearean tragedy, she casually commented, 'Oh, Hamlet? We studied that for our tenth and even performed the play.' Then my schoolteacher mother launched into an elaborate explanation of the complex philosophy in Hamlet that I was struggling with. I used her arguments in my assignment and got an A.

I like to believe that was when our relationship started to change; I began to respect her intelligence; thus far I had resented any form of control that she exercised over my life. After I turned sixteen, I went through a phase where I couldn't wait to become an adult and take my own decisions. I no longer wanted her to rule on how long I should keep my hair, how short I could have my skirt, and what sort of friends were good for me. At some stage—I don't clearly remember when—our relationship changed. I changed. Because I began to see her as my friend and no longer my adversary. But there's time for all that later.

In the winter of 1979, Azuo suddenly began talking about the war days. I had heard some of it from my grandparents when I was quite small. But most of their stories were about the ghosts of young soldiers who came back to haunt the living. Our grandmother would say, 'They were so young, all of them, so terribly young. Of course, they didn't want to die, of course they tried to come back and live their lives over again. People say that the dead revisit the places where they last were in their earthly lives. So, the spirits of the young soldiers have been doing just that.'

The elders were so matter-of-fact about it and people began to identify the spirits according to the territories where they usually made their appearance. For instance, the former Garrison Hill area was known for its battalions of ghost soldiers who would march past to the rhythm of an accompanying band. The occupants of the house never saw anything, but they nightly heard the soldiers marching past their quarters.

A young woman who was crossing the Commonwealth War Cemetery late at night reported that she had seen two figures as tall as the 8-foot cross, deep in conversation. They were both dressed as British officers and one of them was pointing eastward. She turned tail and ran. People began to call them the ghosts of the cross.

An Angami woman had a lover who came to her only by night. A few weeks later she grew very sickly and her relatives commented on her ill health. An aunt who knew of her love affair was suspicious that her sickness might be related to her new relationship. Her aunt instructed her to tie a bit of thread to her lover's clothing when he came on his nightly visit. She did this, and the next morning they traced the thread to the grave of a Sikh soldier.

People adjusted their lives around the soldier-ghost sightings and, down the years, these stories seemed to lose their novelty after being told too many times. But in every generation, children wanted to hear the stories of the war, both those of the soldiers and those of the survivors. It was a period of our history that was of great interest to us. There were many things about British rule that were strange and fascinating. Grandfather had even witnessed hangings of criminals and murderers at the gallows below the North Police station. He said he could never forget the Chakhesang man who was found guilty of murder. As he was being led to the gallows, the man stamped his feet and let out a defiant warrior cry before he was hanged.

My generation was intensely curious about the war. How had the people survived? What was it like to see one's village bombed? What did they eat when there was no food to be found? What was Kohima like with the influx of a huge soldier population? These were the questions we often asked. We were not interested in the military strategies used to oust the Japanese from their positions. But the human struggles that our people endured—those things were more interesting to us. And most important of all, how did they rebuild Kohima after the war? I let Azuo do the telling, feeling fortunate that she wanted to.

'The whole town of Kohima was evacuated and no one was allowed to stay there. But some people defied District Commissioner Charles Pawsey's orders and stayed on in their houses with their elderly parents. There was a widow of Kohima village who saved a Nepali soldier. He was from the Assam Regiment, and his unit had retreated from the fighting in Jessami. He managed to reach Kohima in spite of a leg wound which slowed him down. He had been without food for many days. The elderly widow bathed his wounds and took care of him. They shared whatever food she had in the house as she nursed him back to health. She gave him her husband's clothes to wear as it was dangerous for him to be in his uniform; the Japanese had occupied the village and they routinely ransacked houses looking for food. One day, as luck would have it, two Japanese soldiers came to their house. They roughly demanded food and the widow gestured that there was no food in the house. One of them caught hold of the Nepali and wanted to kill him. But the widow pushed her way in between the two men and shouted that the man was her son. She managed to convince the soldiers and after some time, the Japanese went away without harming him. Some days later, the Nepali man tearfully bid farewell to his "mother" and rejoined his battalion.'

❧

TWO

Remembering 1944

Azuo remembered things in a fragmented manner and her stories were narrated without a beginning, a middle, and an end. You would just have to be around at the right moment to catch the story as it appeared, dredged up from her memory bank, and pondered upon as though it had been another lifetime altogether. She sometimes seemed to doubt that what she was telling us had really happened. She never answered my many questions directly; she simply narrated what she remembered of that time period.

'There was nothing,' she continued the next afternoon as though we had never stopped to eat dinner and gone to sleep and gotten up in the morning. 'There was no food when we came back from Dimapur because all the Marwaris had gone away. The Marwaris who sold groceries in their town shops had all abandoned Kohima so there was no food to be had. DC Pawsey was very angry at this and he banned them from ever returning to Kohima after that incident. But then, how could anyone have stayed on in a town that was being bombed day and night? The Brothers Chakravorty and the owners of Doss & Co., all Bengali traders, also ran off to Dimapur, but they kept their shops open with assistants to look after the shops, so they had no problem in coming back to reopen and carry on their trade.

When we returned after the war, we spent our first night in an abandoned house. Many families did that. The house was in a dilapidated condition, but at least the kitchen had a roof and we could cook food. The five of us joined together the two beds in the bedroom, and we were so exhausted we slept immediately after eating even though the wind was blowing in through holes in the walls. The next morning, we went to find our house and what a shock we got! Nothing was left standing. The place was unrecognisable. There was tin strewn on the ground, and a few burnt planks were all that was left of our house. We cried when we saw the total destruction the war had wrought. Uncle Suohie's house was the only one in the vicinity that was still standing. It was not a big house, but its walls were still intact. They invited us to stay there while we rebuilt our home, and all of us crammed into that little house. We children were excited to be living under the same roof, but Ntsa was greatly embarrassed by the fact that her family would be imposing on our neighbours for a long period of time. She constantly reminded us not to be naughty and to help Uncle Suohie's wife with the fetching of water or wood.

In reality, no house in the village had escaped bombing. Even their house had holes in some of the rooms, but it was possible for the five of us to sleep in two of the beds.

Uncle Suohie's daughter Neiseü was my friend. In the morning, we got up early and excitedly ran off to see the rest of the village. Like us, other people were returning to their homes. We saw several women mourning loudly because they could not find their houses any more. Kohima village was like nothing we had seen before. Most of the houses were gone, and as we went around the ruins, we saw men at work. Some were bringing in posts to make new dwellings, while others were dragging in house materials, such as bamboo and planks, and the women were helping by digging and clearing the debris away.

"Children, don't go that way!" a man warned us when we were about to run past the old British bakery. The British had not removed the corpses of dead Japanese soldiers they had found holed up inside the giant oven. It was from that position that the Japanese had been sniping at enemy soldiers and causing many casualties.

The sight of grown women weeping over their lost homes as though mourning their dead was fascinating for us, and we stood at a distance and stared and stared at them. Afterwards, when I told my mother about it, she chided me saying that it was very hard for those people who had nowhere to shelter; that it was very rude of us to stare at such people. I felt a twinge of shame when she put it that way. But really, we were children, we didn't know better. Nor could we have done anything to help. Some men were clearing away the debris of old thatch, bamboo and wood, while others were disposing of burnt stocks of grain. Every few yards we could see the temporary shelters they had put up to live in while they made new homes.

In the Mission Compound area, there were a few houses that had escaped bombing. The Mission House that had been built by Clark was quite damaged in the war. But the chapel and the mahogany house were still standing. Reverend Supplee conducted English services in the chapel regularly before the village was occupied by the Japanese. We would see soldiers come to church with their rifles at their side. They would lay down their weapons, kneel, and pray before going back to their posts. Reverend Supplee and his family were evacuated to America at the beginning of the war, but when the war was over, they returned to their Naga home.

The little mahogany house with its red roof was used as a school building by the Mission School.

By a miracle, the teacher Rüzhükhrie's house in the Mission area was quite unharmed by the bombing. The few other buildings that survived the bombing were the Jain temple which had been built in the 1920s, and some of the houses that were used by the Marwari traders. These were in the town area. In the village area, there were practically no houses left standing. The ruins of Kohima village were a result of regular bombing by the allied forces. They said it was the only way to get rid of the Japanese who were very firmly entrenched in the village.

The District Commissioner's men did not take long to show up. Even as people were dismantling what was left of their homes and scavenging whatever could be reused, such as nails and screws, DC Pawsey and his men drove up with truckloads of tin and timber. DC Pawsey's Angami assistants set up a table and wrote down the names of all the people who had lost their homes. They went from clan to clan writing down names. Against the names, they wrote down the exact losses suffered by the household, such as loss of grain, houses, and so on. Every family who reported their losses were given new housing material to rebuild. DC Pawsey also distributed some money by way of compensation. The money and sheets of tin were given to all the people with damaged or destroyed houses and granaries. After distributing the tin, the DC's men, in addition, brought bags of ration rice for all the villagers to use. I heard that they did this in every village that was bombed.

It's amazing how, after a war, people scramble to get their lives back to normal. We all did this too, rebuilding homes and beginning the cycle of school and field-going as soon as we could.

We were more fortunate than others because Ntsa found her stock of rice intact. She had hidden two bags of rice and they had somehow escaped being discovered by enemy soldiers. In the garden we found some sour *gazie* leaves that she could put in the broths she made with potatoes and the dried meat that we had brought from the village. So, we were better off than many of our neighbours where food was concerned. The war had lasted so long that people had either finished their stocks of food or had to stand by helplessly as the enemy stole the grain they had laboured so hard to produce. Many people had to depend on the generosity of other villages at this time. Had DC Pawsey not thought of distributing rice, it is likely many of our people would have died of starvation. When the invasion began, we could not till our fields, so there was great anxiety in people's minds. But with the paddy seeds distributed by DC Pawsey, people were able to cultivate their fields again.

There were two major activities that year. The villagers spent the first period after the war rebuilding their houses, and as soon as that was done, they returned to their neglected fields to till them with the new paddy seed. It was a fast-growing variety and everyone called it *rosho lha* as they could not pronounce *ration lha*.

Around then, just before they started the work of rebuilding the village, DC Pawsey approached the elders with a suggestion which he thought they would happily accept. The road engineers had been working with bulldozers that they had brought to Kohima before the war. DC Pawsey told our elders, "If you allow me, I can level the whole village and build a road right through the village."

To his great surprise, all the elders protested and begged him not to do so. Their spokesman said, "*Chaha*, if you do that, we will never be able to make out which are the boundary lines between our clan lands. People will be forever fighting over land. It will not be a good thing at all and we cannot allow you to do that." DC Pawsey respected their decision and said he would at least build a road through the village, which he did. Many elders used to say in the typically jocular manner of the Angamis, "*Hei*, if it wasn't for the Japan war, we wouldn't have gotten this road in our village." DC Pawsey was a typical white man who couldn't fathom that our boundaries depended on the topography of the land and that we used gullies and rocks and formations in the land to mark out the boundaries between clan lands!

Before the war, most houses in the village were made of bamboo and thatch. The thatch roofs were quite flammable, and if a house caught fire, it was only a matter of time in which the next houses would go up in flames. It was almost impossible to save the old houses. After the war, everyone used tin roofing, and it prevented houses being so easily destroyed by fire. Many years before the war, there was a mentally unstable man in the village. One afternoon, he discovered that most people had gone to the fields leaving the village nearly empty. It was during one of the busiest periods of the agricultural year. That man began to burn house after house before he was caught. People were out in the fields when they saw thick columns of black smoke rising from the village. When they realised what was happening, all of them ran back. By then it was too late and many lost their homes. With the houses made of tin, that risk of all the clan houses burning down is not very likely, but people make their houses too close together so that is not good.

As life was slowly picking up again, DC Pawsey encouraged those Nagas who wanted to become traders to start their own shops. Before the war, the main market was in an area called Manipuri Market run by Manipuri traders. It was the first marketplace in the town and it was under the protection of the British garrison. After the war, shops were built along the Mission road. Neilasa was one of the first Angamis to become a trader. He opened a hardware store. There were a number of stores selling hardware. These stores were very popular after the war with so many people rebuilding their homes.

'The two Bengali shops, Doss and Co. and Chakravorty, were departmental stores. When the shops reopened, people felt very happy as it was a sign of normalcy. We bought whatever food they were selling and were quite assured the war was behind us now.

In 1953, Dr Neilhouzhü Kire opened the first pharmacy in Kohima. He received patients who came from far off villages with all kinds of ailments. He was a kind of emergency doctor who performed stitching of injuries at his pharmacy. In those days, the doctor was even required to stand in as a dentist when the need arose.

Though there were a number of new shops, it was nothing like what you see today. Gradually, shops were opened considering the needs of the customers. The very first bookshop in town was opened by Benjamin Sekhose. He supplied all the school textbooks besides stationery material, Bibles, hymn books, and calendars. Tailoring shops and bakery shops came much later, and as the shops increased, the perimeter of the town kept growing until it reached the TCP gate. Jadial Sekhose was a good baker; he baked cakes and bread and sold them from his home. Eventually the Kohima Bakery was opened, owned by Kelakieü and her husband, Ashim Roy. By the late forties and early fifties the shops that you see now were establishing themselves and becoming part of the life of the town.'

THREE

Rebuilding

The pungent smell of food filled the kitchen and Azuo paused in her narration as we gravitated towards the fireplace so that she could serve us the warm rice and *galho* made of dried mustard leaves, garlic, strips of meat, and red sorrel leaves. It was spiced with chili and red chili flakes floated up on my plate. Winter food. The chili kept you warm and protected against colds. But I had never developed a liking for chili and I took out as much as I could of the flakes. I took the ladle and stirred the pot, an action that pushed the chili to the side and enabled me to scoop out the grey coloured soup. Azuo was a good cook and she insisted on making the food herself. My schoolwork kept me very busy, so I welcomed the arrangement.

Smoke from the hearth found its way out and danced over our heads. The kitchen walls were darkened by wood smoke, but Azuo adamantly continued cooking food on a wood fire because, according to her, it tasted better. The gas stove was for boiling milk and making tea, or cooking daal and rice.

Over the fire hung bunches of chives, garlic, basil, and some maize still in their jackets. The wood for the kitchen was drying above the fireplace, long fibres of soot dropping off the longer pieces.

In the months after my father's death, it used to seem like everything had come to a standstill in our family house. Azuo rarely went into the big sitting room where two picture frames of her and my father dominated the shelf. I would tiptoe in and find layers of dust on the mantelpiece. I took upon myself the task of hiding a flannel cloth in a corner with which I dusted the room two or three times a week. In the first of the two photographs, they were smiling back happily. Azuo had her hair caught up at the back and a few curls had escaped, framing a pretty face. My father looked sombre in a white shirt and loose tie. He was holding a guitar. They must have been in their twenties. How very young they both looked. So different from what they looked like in later life as I knew them. The second photograph was a close-up of the two of them. Many times, I have looked at the photographs and thought, these can't be my parents; they look like they could have been my classmates.

There was another photograph as well. It was Christmas. My father was holding up my five-year-old brother so he could touch the angel on top of the tree. They were both laughing. That was also the last Christmas with my father. He died on the 2nd of January after getting dreadfully sick on New Year's Eve. My brother Ato and I were bundled off to my grandmother's house that night as the ambulance came to get him. In the morning, Atsa took us to the hospital to see him, but he couldn't speak. There were tubes everywhere

and my eyes filled up with tears before I could stop myself.
Dad gave me a weak smile and signalled me to come closer.
He took my hand and squeezed it and nodded towards my
brother. I understood. *Look after him.* That was what the look
meant and the squeeze on my hand was only for me. *I love you,
my girl.* We had to go after that as the nurse said he was too
weak to be allowed visitors. I remember thinking, *but we are
not visitors, we are his children.* Of course, I didn't say anything. I
took my brother's hand and distracted him with a sweet and
we followed Atsa back to her house.

Azuo became a widow in 1971. The headstone on my
father's grave reads,

Mengutuolie Angami
Beloved father and husband
1932–1971

I think I blamed my mother for my father's premature
death. In the perverse manner that a child can often adopt, I
blamed her for marrying him even when she knew he had a
heart condition and that the doctor had said he might not live
beyond his thirtieth year. In the end he made it to his thirty-
ninth birthday. Still, I blamed her for bringing widowhood
upon herself and depriving us of a father when we were so
young. I blamed her for not marrying another man instead
of my sickly Dad, a man who could not be with us through
our growing-up years. I blamed her for the loneliness that
would overwhelm me—though I couldn't understand why,
every time I looked for him in his study and found only his
empty chair.

As for her, she withdrew into a shell and grew old instantly. At 37, her hair turned grey overnight. She took leave from her job as a teacher for a whole year in which she did nothing but mope around the house, forgot to feed us, and kept sending us off to Atsa Bonuo's house. I could not help feeling that when my father died, I lost my mother too. It was as though she couldn't be bothered to be a mother anymore.

One night, I woke up and heard her talking to someone in the room. It was pitch dark outside and I knew the maid would be fast asleep by now. Who could she be talking to? It took a few seconds for me to realise that she was talking to my father in that loving tone they used only for each other. I froze and lay very quiet. Stealthily, I made a little opening in my blanket and peered through it to look at my father, but there was no one. My mother must have sensed that I was awake because she stopped speaking after that and climbed back into bed. We never talked about that, not once.

It was her sister, Azuo Zeü, who finally took matters in hand and sat her down to talk some sense into her.

'These children need a mother, not a grandmother or an aunt. We don't mind helping out at all. They are good children. But they need you to be a parent to them. Look, Khonuo, I am sorry to sound harsh, but you have spent the whole year mourning Mengutuolie. No one will criticise you if you go back to your job and start earning for the family. You are still young. You can't retreat from life like this.'

She protested a bit, but in the end, she went back to work and life was a little easier after that. The income from my mother's teaching job put me through High School and covered part of my college education. My brother Ato was still in Class 7 the year I began to attend college. The first two years at college were a struggle for me as everything was very new; but by the time I was in my first year BA, I had got the hang of it.

❧

Azuo had cleared the pots when I was taking our empty plates over to the sink.

'When did you go back to school?' I re-opened our conversation as I sat down.

'Oh, not for some months. School was not an immediate priority for the government in that period.'

'But surely they were concerned about reopening the school?'

'Yes, they were, of course. They were not the only ones. Educated men were worried about the young students wandering around for want of a school to attend. The missionary family had left for America at the beginning of the war. They were still away even when the government declared that the war was over. The situation led Mr Neiliehu Belho and Mr Vibeilie Belho to open a school so that school-going children would stop losing so many days of study. We sat in makeshift sheds and did our lessons. They didn't run it for long as DC Pawsey quickly appointed some teachers and restarted the Mission School.

It was only in the month of August that arrangements were made for Classes 3 to 6 to return to school. The teachers taught us English and Mathematics as we sat in temporary classrooms. It brought back memories of the weeks before the war, how we used to run out of the classrooms to hide in the trenches whenever we heard the sirens. The trenches were all filled up now. The fighter planes and sirens were a part of our recent past. Our parents had expected us to be exultant at going back to school. However, not everybody felt the same. My older sister and her friends did not want to go back to their studies.

"Aren't we too old?" sister Zeü had asked Father, and since she had turned 15 and had already studied half a year in Class 6, Father allowed her to go to nursing school without going back to regular school. Zeü and three of her friends joined nursing school in Shillong. After a year, Zeü qualified to be a midwife and she came back home.

There was another group of big girls who did not rejoin school. Since there was no question of forcing anyone to attend school, those girls stayed at home, helping their parents with house work and field work. After the missionaries returned, they consulted with the female teachers in the school, and together they thought up a plan of teaching the older girls to bake cake. Their instructor was the wife of the other missionary called Tanquist. Mrs Tanquist was a big-built woman, a hard worker. She was very strict with the girls, even if they were no longer at school. Not only would they learn to bake, they would also learn to converse in English and pray a short prayer. It was called the 'one-minute-prayer' and was designed to help the girls to speak English. Every evening, after the baking class was over, she assembled the girls in a group and made them pray. Mrs Tanquist always knew whose turn it was. She would take out her register of names and call out, 'Neiseü, you will begin the prayer tonight.'

Neiseü would blush and stammer as she began her prayer. 'Dear Heavenly Father, thank you for… for…' she would stammer as she desperately sought for the appropriate English words to finish her sentence. Mrs Tanquist would step in at this moment and supply the words, 'thank you for the nice time we have had.' If the girls continued to stumble, the missionary lady would continue to help them with more sentences, 'Bless my friends and bless my family. Bless my land and bless us all. In Jesus' name. Amen.' All the other girls joined in the amen loudly.

The girls looked forward to the baking class as cakes had become very popular, but they dreaded the one-minute prayer time. Some girls would not utter a word when it was their turn, not even to repeat what the missionary lady was praying. So, it was quite frustrating for the missionary lady. Nevertheless, it all ended well and cake-baking became the new skill that a young woman could lay claim to when she set up her own home. There were no baking ovens then, and it was the men who discovered that the abandoned ammunitions boxes could be very good for baking. They got hold of them and tried them out and found that they worked very well. It was a very convenient arrangement and there were enough such boxes available.'

I knew the ammunitions box Azuo was talking about. In my childhood, nearly every household in Kohima had one such box for baking cake. At Christmas or weddings, the women would bring out their ammunition boxes and warm them on a slow fire while other members of the family helped to beat the batter. The box stood in a corner of the kitchen when not in use. I connected it to all the memories Azuo was sharing with me.

'The older girls got married one by one as there was nothing more to do in life. The few who did not marry went on to nursing school and came back to work in the hospital. They too got married and had children and continued to work as nurses or midwives with their long working hours and irregular shifts. The jobs paid good money so they were reluctant to give them up.

We now had a new headmaster at school as the Supplees had finally left the Naga Hills. It was around this time that our people intensified their protest over our areas being made part of the new Indian nation. In retaliation, the government of India ordered all American missionaries to leave the country as soon as possible. The Supplees were amongst the last families to leave in 1949. The Reverend Supplee was a musician who had written songs on Kohima which were sung by different generations of Nagas in later years. During their stay in Kohima, Ruth Supplee, the missionary's wife, was frequently sick and would spend days confined to her bed. Many people were sad to see them go. When they had returned after the war, people saw no reason for them to leave again so soon. They had become such a part of our community, so the government's orders came as a big shock. Tearfully, both old and young bid them goodbye when the day came.

Despite that major interruption, our schooling was continued with new local teachers. Lhuviniu Lungalang was the new headmaster. Our school had been upgraded to a

High School, so our batch attended school regularly until the tenth; the following year, we sat for our matriculation exams and when the results were declared, our headmaster was very pleased. He announced that the school had finally got a hundred per cent pass result.

Ours was not the only school at the time. There was an Assamese school too, but no one we knew went to that school. Before the war, a businessman named John Angami started a school in the Viswema village area in 1936 so that students in the southern villages did not have to travel as far as Kohima to get an education. It was called the John Institute and DC Pawsey was very pleased with such initiatives from the local people.

In our generation, our parents encouraged us to study, especially since they had themselves been educated in the Mission schools. They knew very well that education offered a better life and wanted us to reap the advantages of western education. Many of our teachers were well trained and they demanded a high level of dedication from us. They would encourage us to dream big, saying that nothing was out of our reach if we would work hard at it. We believed every word they said.

We left school in 1953, but the headmaster invited some of us back to work as trainee teachers. That was how my career as a teacher first began. I didn't go to college. To have a matriculate degree was quite enough in those days. My best friend Lydia and I joined the school together as junior teachers. My other friend Neiseü had stopped studying by then, and we saw less and less of each other. Lydia and I had been friends from nursery, we were neighbours and we were inseparable. But her family moved to Dimapur after her brother James was killed. Then on, it became hard to see each other frequently. Her husband's family are from Dimapur too, so our meetings took place on her visits up here but only after a lapse of many months. Some of the boys who were in our batch enrolled in Engineering and Veterinary Science courses. It was such a big thing in our days if the boys could do well in Mathematics and qualify for these lines of study.'

FOUR

Azuo's Family Life

Azuo's parents were still alive when Father died. They didn't live far from us and she made it a point to visit them almost every day, sometimes spending the night at their house if it was the weekend. We liked our grandfather well enough but Ato and I agreed that our grandmother was a little strange. We called her Atsa Bonuo. As we grew up, we were warned not to ask her about her second son, the uncle we never knew. When he turned seven, Ami Razou became very sick. He had a very high fever and none of the medicines or cures worked on him. He died within two days of contracting the fever. Atsa Bonuo never recovered from his death. Azuo told us that for many years she would talk about him as if he were still alive. When new people visited and asked how many children she had, she always replied, 'I have two daughters and two sons.'

If they asked what the children were doing she would explain what the older boy and the girls were doing. If the visitors persisted with their questions and asked what the younger boy was doing, she would say 'nothing'. They would be surprised but too polite to ask more. It being a small town, they eventually learned that the younger son had died years before. Atsa Bonuo also had this strange habit of examining us minutely, one by one and commenting, 'Just like Razou at your age.' Ato and I felt as though we knew him although neither of us had ever seen him. He became our secret playmate and sometimes when we played ball, we would pretend Razou had kicked the ball downhill, and we would race out into the street to fetch it.

Atsa Bonuo always made a lot of food. Her kitchen had an earthen floor which she kept very clean by rubbing it with new mud once a week. The sink stood in the corner at the end of the kitchen where all the washing was done. The whole interior of the kitchen was very dark. There was a small window overlooking the garden. It faced east and was the only source of light. Atsa Bonuo kept a kerosene lamp near her seat and would light it when she came to the kitchen. In their house, when night fell, our grandparents used lanterns that threw long shadows on the walls. As the wick burned, the shadows moved constantly. Ato used to be very frightened of them. He thought they were spirits. Azuo laughed when I told her about it. She had been happy growing up in that house.

'Becoming a working girl was one of the greatest joys of my life. For the first time, I was earning money and making a living for myself. I could buy things for the house and go shopping for clothes and shoes with Lydia. I even bought meat for the house and your grandmother told me that I should start saving my salary to build a house in future. I thought Ntsa was joking! Our house was not very big but there were enough rooms for us all. When it was rebuilt, your grandfather added two extra bedrooms saying that all of us would need our own rooms. He was right because Zeü did not care to share a room with me after she had finished her training. There were two sitting rooms, the first one was quite plain and was for regular guests. The second one was dimly lit and we kept our sofa set with the velvet covers in there; it was used only when we had people like the headmaster visiting, or an official from the government.

The kitchen was built in the same spot as before. But it is much smaller than the original kitchen. The leftover space was converted into another kitchen for guests. You know your grandparents used to have many guests earlier. Theirs was a big house and Ntsa had several relatives from her village visiting Kohima. Even if they were not family members, she would not turn them away knowing that they had no other place to go to. When Nzuo Zeü got married, we did most of the cooking outside in the back garden as the two kitchens were too small. The men brought logs of wood and made temporary fireplaces to cook pots of rice and meat.

'It was one of the first weddings after the war and people were happy to have something to celebrate. Nzuo Zeü was still very young, about 16 when she got married the following year. Her best friend bought her a pair of white sandals as a wedding gift. Another friend gifted her a belt! Even though the shops had reopened, in the early days all that they sold was food, utensils, and yarn. With the Marwari traders gone, some men from Kohima village ventured to open yarn stores where they also sold soap and groceries on the side. But no one had ever heard of gifting a bride with yarn. It was more usual to weave her either a body-cloth or a waist-cloth. Nzuo Zeü received about four such cloths. Her husband's side of the family brought baskets of grain to his house. The guests teased them saying they would have enough *rosho lha* to last them the first year of their lives together.

Our older brother Amo was still working for the army. He had joined before the war. He took a few days' leave from work and stayed home during Zeü's wedding. Your uncle Razou was six years old when Amo joined the army. When he got some leave, Amo came home looking very smart in his Assam Regiment uniform. When he joined the army at the end of 1942, Amo was just 16, but he was tall for his age and had the muscles of a man so he could pass for an 18-year old. Rumours were rife that the Japanese could invade at any time, and the army needed every man who wanted to be recruited.

'Razou was determined then to become a soldier just like his big brother Amo. He would march around the house carrying a little toy gun made of wood which Amo had made, singing a popular marching song the British army soldiers used to sing. Grown-ups would tease him and call him "soldier-boy" and salute when he passed by. No one suspected he would be dead in less than a year. It was so unexpected. Ntsa was still grieving over Razou in her peculiar way when Zeü's wedding came by. But she had to set her sorrow aside and concentrate on her daughter's marriage. After the wedding, she resumed mourning Razou again.

But at least during the wedding week, everyone felt a sense of peace: the war was over, people had new houses and life was beginning to become normal again. They felt as though the worst was surely behind them. We were all happy at Zeü's marriage. It was the best combination of a traditional marriage and a church wedding. The couple were blest by the pastor in church where they exchanged their vows, but the wedding feast was conducted in the traditional manner with meat shares for all the paternal uncles and a generous share for the bride's age-mates.'

FIVE

Azuo and Ami Amo

'I didn't marry until fourteen years later. By then, everyone was convinced I was going to end up a spinster. Zeü's son, Vilhou, would ask me every year if I was going to get married in that year. I always answered him with a maybe, but he too got tired of asking when many years went by and I remained unmarried. Nmi Amo was the only person who didn't tease me. He said I shouldn't worry about finding a husband, and that he would take care of me on his army pension.

I had my own income as I still had my job as a teacher at the Mission School. Some years later, the headmaster called me to his office. He said he was pleased with my work and informed me that from then on, I would be regularised as the History teacher. The school moved to its new location at High School colony and more teachers were hired. At first, my fellow teachers teased me whenever a new single male teacher would join. It was done in a good-natured way and we would all laugh together. Then your father came home, having finished his studies, and we met and it was clear from the first time we saw each other that we were meant to be together.

Yet people opposed our marriage. My aunt Ania Nisoü came and warned, "He has a weak heart. Doctors have said he won't live long." My other aunt said, "That man was supposed to have died when he was a schoolboy. You are courting widowhood if you decide to go ahead with this marriage." All the opposition only made us adamant nothing would part us. We went ahead with our marriage and we managed to have twelve wonderful years together. We never fought, not even one day. We made each day count.'

Besides my father's premature death, a death in the family that was really hard for me was my uncle Amo's. It took me years to ask the question 'Why did Ami Amo die?'

Ato and I were very small when Ami Amo was rushed to hospital one afternoon. He was a favourite with us because when he visited, he would play with us for hours instead of wasting time indoors talking to our parents. We couldn't believe it when he died the same evening. I was seven years old, Ato was just two and a half. We really had no idea what death was. At least I knew that when someone died, you didn't get to see the dead person anymore. That made me very sad at the time as I really liked uncle Amo, and didn't want to stop seeing him.

'He had a war wound that never really healed,' Azuo had explained. 'It was a splinter that had lodged very close to his heart. Doctors said it was too dangerous to operate. They did cut him open and then they stitched him up again without doing anything, saying they would not be able to stop the bleeding. He had steadfastly refused to marry, knowing his condition. He always knew he might suddenly die if the splinter punctured the aorta. That was what happened the day he was rushed to hospital with profuse bleeding. He was 39 when he died.'

'Oh, I thought he was much younger. He always looked so young and happy when he played with Ato and me. I remember how he would make us look for him all over the house while he hid in the closet or in the big wooden trunk.'

Talking about him and getting to know more about him always had its own power to heal the scars I had carried from childhood over this particular loss. As I grew older, I felt more confident to ask the questions that I had so wanted answers to. What had he been like with other people? Had they also liked him as much as we did? And did they miss him as much? Azuo tried to answer as best as she could.

'He loved you two very much. Amo had the heart of a child. He made people glad wherever he went. He was just very loving and understanding and would stick up for me whenever Zeü and I fought. When we were on our own, he would remind me to be more respectful to Zeü because she was older by at least five years. Nzuo Zeü used to be very bossy and would insist that I do things her way. Ntsa allowed her to choose my clothes and shoes, and even to cut my hair! Once she cut my hair so short in front that I could not go to school for a week. That was the only time she said sorry. She persuaded me to wear a woollen hat to school until my hair grew out again. I had to do that as I had already missed so much school. Back then, if you were really sick, everyone got to know about it as there were only two doctors and all the families in our colony went to them. If you were not sick and had missed school for more than ten days, you would get an explanation call and a warning. After that, any more absences without a medical reason would end in your expulsion from school.

So, I went to school with the woollen hat and got teased mercilessly by the boys. They spent recess chasing me and trying to pull off my hat. My best friend Lydia took one peek and said I needn't worry because my hair had started to grow back, and it didn't look as bad as on the first day. I think Amo always knew that Nzuo Zeü was a bit of a bully, and he tried to protect me without letting her see he was on my side. I looked on her as a surrogate mother because my mother grew very distant after Razou died. As I was growing older, I took Zeü's advice on clothes and on friendships. She decided which friends I should keep and which girls I should avoid. Mind you, she was usually quite shrewd where people were concerned. Two of the friends she warned me away from were great gossips. They were the source of a lot of gossip in town that broke up friendships and even families.

'She was dead against me curling my hair like many of the girls in our batch were doing. In my wedding photographs you see me with long shoulder-length, straight hair. After you came along, it was difficult to manage long hair and my colleague, Sanuo, gave me a haircut and a "permanent", as we used to call it. It was a long process and the chemicals used for curling hair smelt so awful. But you know all about it. You have seen me do it often enough. I loved the results well enough to endure the treatment.'

'What was Azuo Zeü's reaction?'

'Oh, she didn't like it much. But she didn't say anything, after all I was a married woman and could do what I wanted.' She laughed at the memory and looked quite merry.

'She has changed over the years, in fact she has changed a lot after her husband's death. You used to ask why she always sends us food. It is her way of showing that she cares for us. That's what many of our people do. When they want to express their affection, they bring you gifts of food. We are very awkward with showing love for another person. At funerals, we don't know how to ask how the bereaved persons are feeling. Instead, we keep asking them to eat some food. Making food for the family becomes our way of showing them sympathy and a way to partake in their sorrow. It's a strange custom and sometimes when you are grieving, it can be annoying to be asked by many different people to eat food. That is the last thing you want to do. You have no appetite just then and eating would seem like a betrayal. It would feel as though your sorrow is only skin-deep. But for the person offering food, it is an act of love and they try to persuade you to eat and stay strong so you can experience the whole process of the funeral. "You need to stay strong and keep him company the whole day," that is the excuse they give to make you eat. But why are we talking so much about death? Ah, it is because you asked about Nmi Amo.

You know, there are days when I still miss Amo a lot. He was so kind, so loving and so good. No one could have been that good. He must have been sent to us for a purpose. To teach us to be kind to each other? Maybe. Ntsa was quite heartbroken when he died. It was many years after Razou's death; still, it's very hard when your children die before you. It was not just Ntsa. The rest of us were devastated. We had lived our lives with the knowledge that he would not live to be old, but when it came, it was still such a shock. There he was—a vibrant, lovely young man who everyone loved—and suddenly he was dead and lying in a coffin. It was unreal, unacceptable. But death is always unacceptable.

'Earlier, when I used to take flowers to his grave on Easter morning, I used to sense very acutely that he might suddenly appear before me smiling happily, as he always used to do. It was enough to send a shiver through me when I went alone, especially if there was no one else at the graveyard that early. It's many years now since I have been there. My knees are so wobbly now; climbing up the steps is somehow manageable but climbing down has become so difficult for me. I wouldn't like to fall down those steps and break something. I know he will understand.'

'Did he have a girlfriend? A girl he loved but could not marry?' I had to ask.

Azuo looked thoughtful. She tried hard to remember before she slowly replied,

'I don't think he had a special girlfriend as such. Many girls loved him. He was good to look at, and he was kind and polite. Amo occupied a special place in our colony. He was our war hero. He had been decorated for his courage in the Second World War, and he had two medals. One was for his role in leading an attack on a post occupied by the Japanese. His group managed to kill the enemy and recapture the guns in that position. But you rarely saw him wearing his war medals like the older soldiers would at festivals and special days. He preferred to keep them in his trunk along with his military papers.

Certainly, there were young women who wanted to marry him, but he never got close to any of them. He treated all of them with great respect, in a brotherly fashion, and none of the women felt offended by this. As a matter of fact, they banded together and started calling themselves "Amo's wives". They became quite pally with each other, and would do things for him, like weaving new cloths or knitting him hats in the cold weather. Even when they married other men in later life, some of them would send him gifts of food and would ask about his welfare. It was quite unusual and very touching. The marvellous thing was, the husbands knew about it and thought it was girlish fun and did not try to stop them. He was, in every sense, everyone's hero. The husbands of these young women had also looked up to Nmi Amo in their time.'

I could not imagine a scenario like that ever coming to pass in my time. Azuo read my mind. 'People were more broad-minded in our days. You might find that hard to believe, seeing as we dress in such an old-fashioned way. But it's not about clothes. I guess people were more tolerant, more understanding and less quick to judge than they are today. Ours is a generation that has seen the devastation of war. We are people who know what it's like to lose everything almost overnight, homes, loved ones, and life as we knew it before the war. When death is so imminent, some things in life simply stop being important. Some things become bigger, and small things turn insignificant. That is what war does. Love in all its different aspects comes into play during wartime. You can experience romantic love, and you can also experience brotherly love, the kind that comes to the forefront between two humans when death is very close at hand.

'I think war makes people more generous and more benevolent than peace. I don't mean that war is a good thing. It can also bring out the worst in people. The way the enemy soldiers were scrambling for food and taking away whatever they could get from the villagers was awful to see. We also witnessed that there were people reluctant to share their food, but in the midst of all that, there were widows who went around to check if everyone in their camp had got food. If they found a family with lots of small children, they would readily share their food with them. It was a strange time: we saw some people doing the meanest things and we saw others doing the most noble of actions.

'When Amo died, many people came to help in the funeral. While the women mourned him loudly, the men divided themselves into two groups. The first group brought wood and made a very fine coffin, and the second group took turns to dig the grave and carve the wooden cross with his name and date of birth and death. They made sure he was given a grand funeral befitting the life he had lived. I still remember what the pastor said.

"Amo Molhoulie lived a hero's life, not only on the battlefield, but even after the war was over. I saw him grow up as an active little boy who was very energetic, taking part in all the activities arranged for his age-mates. He was a good wrestler and sportsman. He was a very obedient son. There was only one time that he did not obey his parents, and that was when he insisted on becoming a soldier. That was his heart's desire and neither of his parents could stop him from fulfilling his dream. You might all know that he was wounded in the war, but not before he earned a medal for his great courage. After he returned, he could not take on a full-time job, but he created his own job in the village. He made the elderly feel cared for, he attended to widows and members of the community who were in need, and spent time fixing their homes and barns. He took out time for the children and played with them and created good memories with them. We all learned from him what real heroes are like."

'There was not a dry eye at the burial when the pastor finished speaking. The whole year, people kept bringing flowers to his grave, removing the faded ones and replacing them with new offerings. Do you remember the first grave was a mound in the ground with bamboo fencing? We replaced that with a concrete memorial the following year.'

'I remember the funeral,' I said. 'I was very young and I cried a lot, and Ato cried because he saw me crying. Both you and Azuo Zeü were surrounded by people. We couldn't come near you and we felt even more sad because of that. Two big girls came and pulled us away whenever we tried to come to you. In the end, we gave up trying and Ato stopped crying and fell asleep.'

'Oh, it was one of the saddest days of our lives, after Razou's death. Amo had been so healthy for so long that we forgot he had a condition. It was like death had forgotten all about him, only to return and snatch him up! And we were oblivious to anything except our grief at losing him. Do you remember who the girls were who looked after you?'

'No. I didn't know their names. They were probably some relatives of ours. They would tell us not to disturb you and pull us away every time we came near the room where they had kept Ami Amo's body. I remember feeling very sad on account of that.'

'I think they were worried we would be as affected as Ntsa was. She kept fainting and had to be revived again and again until the doctor ordered her to be carried to the bedroom where he kept her sedated. They woke her only a few minutes before the funeral. The next few days, she had to be monitored as she was so ill they thought there would soon be another funeral in the house. Miraculously, she recovered and got better. She told us that she had dreamed of Amo; that he was standing in a beautiful garden and waving to her. When she started to run to him, she found there was a river blocking her way. Amo shouted, 'Mother, don't come now! Wait for your time. You won't have to wait long. Look, Razou is here too!' and when she looked up, she saw Razou waving at her.

She woke up shouting for her sons. But when she had quietened down, she said she had seen the most beautiful place and that she would soon go there herself. That dream helped your grandmother to recover and she didn't have to wait long before she joined the two people she loved so much.'

SIX

More Deaths

Atsa died when I was 13, three years after my father had gone. I didn't feel terribly sad as I had expected to be at her death. It just felt right. She was more there than here; she missed her sons so much that I was almost relieved when she finally died. Ato and I never got much attention from her except when we did or said something that reminded her of Razou. Then she would pull us close and look at us keenly and whisper as if to herself, 'So much like Razou,' before she released us.

When she was still around, Ato and I made up a special game where I dressed up like Atsa by covering my head with a scarf, and I would stop the game at any given point, grab his arm and peer into his face repeating the words, 'So much like Razou at your age.' That left us in peals of laughter. When Azuo found out what we were doing, she gave us a sound scolding, saying it was cruel of us to do that. 'Ntsa loved him very much, can't you understand that?' We felt terribly guilty and begged for forgiveness. In time, the memories of these people faded; they'd come back only when I came across an old photograph or an object that belonged to one of them. Then it would feel very strange that they had once been part of my life, that Ato and I had played so happily with Ami Amo and loved him so much, and now there was not even a little bit of him left. I prayed at such moments to let there be a heaven where I would meet him again. And I would remember Atsa's dream of seeing him in a garden of flowers and I would be very sure there was a heaven where Ami Amo had gone to live the rest of his life.

'Sometimes death comes as a mercy,' Azuo looked at me in a strange way. 'I mean that for a person like your grandmother, life had no more meaning when she lost both her sons. She could not wait to be reunited with them and every passing day without them was just torture for her. You know that in the last year of her life, she was no longer functional. She was not even what we would consider old; she was just 63. But she was no longer in touch with reality. I remember she would leave the pot on the fire and forget to put anything in it. That happened several times until Nzuo Zeü got them two girls who did all the cooking and all the housework. In addition, the girls took care of Ntsa and followed her around to make sure she did not fall and hurt herself. Ntsa died of a broken heart. I have heard people say such a thing, but it was only when I saw how Ntsa was so affected by the deaths of Amo and Razou to the point where she wished herself dead, I understood that it was true indeed that some people can die of a broken heart.

We wanted her around, of course, but she was so absent from this world that it became a great burden for your grandfather and us, her remaining children. In the end, when she died, I felt it was a merciful thing and I thanked God in secret for it. This is the first time I am telling anyone about this.' She looked at me sharply as if to warn me not to tell anyone. I understood. After all, it was almost blasphemous to say that a parent's death was a great mercy. But I knew what she meant.

I had been old enough to understand that Atsa would never be the same and she had been simply going from bad to worse every day that passed. The constant care that she required was a strain on other members of her family. It was not safe to leave her alone in the house. It was worse if she wandered out into town. She could not remember where she was and she had trouble finding her way back to the house. It was like living with a two-year-old child whose movements had to be monitored all the time. In that period, Azuo looked exhausted and Azuo Zeü looked even older than Atsa. I tried my best to help, but Atsa was a big woman and I could not stop her when she decided to go off somewhere on her own. She needed coaxing and a firm manner, and that was beyond 13-year-old me. In the end, as Azuo put it, it was a mercy that death came for her.

Strangely, Apuotsa died a year later. That was most unexpected. The girls who had been hired to look after Atsa were still working in the house. One morning they came to call Azuo very worriedly saying that Apuotsa had not woken up that morning. They had both tried to wake him, but he continued to lie curled up in bed and did not respond at all. Azuo hurried over to the house and found her father beyond help. He had died in the night and no one knew. Apuotsa's death was hard for both Ato and me. We were very fond of him and he liked our visits. He was a quiet man and had been overshadowed by his wife most of his life. He was only 65 and had been quite actively looking after Atsa in her final years. No one had realised how lonely he'd become after her death. We used to visit him regularly, but we never knew how deeply he was grieving.

'Apuo, how are you?' Every time Azuo asked him that question, he would smile and reply, 'I'm fine, don't you worry. I am just fine.' He was three years older than Atsa, but of the two of them, he had always been more active, fond of pottering about in the back garden where we would find him replacing old fences and planting saplings. Apuotsa had studied till the fourth standard and worked as a clerk under the British government. He had been an avid collector of newspapers and in a corner of the parlour, old issues of *The Assam Tribune* and *Amrita Bazar Patrika* were piled up in rows. The local newspaper, *Ura Mail*, stood beside the other two papers in a small pile. They had been sorted out according to the years of publication. The bundles of newspapers were tied with jute string and lovingly arranged in a corner. On Saturdays when we visited them, he would take out a bundle, untie it, and show us some historically significant news that he had underlined with a pen. He said it was the mark of an educated person to read newspapers and acquire historical knowledge. These hobbies had kept him busy and content. But after his wife's death, he lost interest in his newspaper collection, and his neat little world began to come apart in a manner that was quite irreparable.

'Was he sick? Did he complain of any pain?' Azuo had minutely questioned the older girl, but she said no to all her questions. Apuotsa had eaten his dinner, and complaining of a headache, had gone to bed early. The girls had not suspected anything so they didn't think it was important to inform my mother who lived close by. Since they were quite young, they were very frightened at what had happened. The older girl burst out crying and could not be comforted. The younger girl began to cry too. In the end, Azuo had to calm them and assure them it was not their fault that Apuotsa had died while they were in the house, and that they should now help her to prepare the house to receive visitors for the funeral. He was buried that same day towards evening. It was not uncommon to have the funeral in the afternoon hours if the person had died the night before.

When Apuotsa died, a terrible silence fell over the whole house: the sudden kind of silence that darkness brings. It was as though all the lights had been put out in the house. We went around speaking in whispers, but we needn't have bothered. It was so quiet and we were not likely to disturb anyone now. I have never known that in any other house. It was like the very life of the house had come to an end. Even after people began to stream in to mourn his passing, I could still hear the deep silence that had fallen over the house.

Some of our male relatives stayed for about a week 'to keep the dead company,' as they said. When they left, there was nothing to do but to lock the house.

'Someday Ato can live in it with his family,' Azuo remarked. I could tell Ato did not like the idea at all.

'Why should I go and live there alone? I want to raise my children in this house,' he said defiantly.

'It's just a manner of speaking. You are the man of the

house now, so you will inherit your father's house as well as your grandfather's house,' Azuo said, trying to placate him.

'Well, I don't need two houses. In any case, Apuotsa's house should go to Vilhou, shouldn't it? He is older than me.'

'Oh, Vilhou's father is a rich man. They will have enough houses for him. In any case the ancestral house is for the youngest son, and since Nmi Amo had no children at all, you could inherit it,' Azuo replied. But she could see that Ato was not ready for the idea and she quickly changed the subject. From time to time, Azuo and Azuo Zeü would go and clean their ancestral house. Traditionally, Ami Amo's descendants would have inherited the house, but since he never married, he had made a will saying he wished it to stay in the family and be inherited by his sister's children. Azuo and Azuo Zeü did discuss the idea of renting it out but could never bring themselves to do that.

'Perhaps we could allow some of Apuo's relatives to use the house without paying rent,' Azuo had suggested. But they both had to agree it was a bad idea as then no one would be responsible for any damage to the house, and since the whole idea was to get someone to live there to maintain it, keeping non-paying boarders was not a good idea. Eventually, they agreed to open it up for family events when one of the children got married, and space was needed for out-of-town relatives. It worked well. During Vilhou's wedding, some family members came with their brood of seven children and they were easily accommodated in our grandparents' house. The kitchen was used to cook the wedding food and the sight of children running in and out the house made it seem like old times again. As I watched them I thought the tall girl chasing her younger brother could almost be me and Ato playing in Apuotsa's house. Only, I was much older now and so was Ato, and Apuotsa and Atsa were no longer there in their usual places in the kitchen. It was a sobering thought.

The house was closed after the wedding, but now it became easier to find excuses to open it again for some event or other. We seemed to have more relatives than ever before visiting Kohima, and Azuo and Azuo Zeü were only too happy to host them in the ancestral house. So, it came to pass quite naturally that Apuotsa's house was repaired and kept clean for family guests. The male relatives would look for things to mend in the house, and they did a good job of it. The female relatives used the kitchen happily, cooking big meals that they shared with the rest of us, their way of expressing gratitude for giving them a free place to stay and cook their own food. It was only people without any relatives who went to eat in the town hotels that sold pork, rice, and boiled mustard leaves. We were not sure where those people stayed when they came to Kohima, probably in some of the dark, dingy town hotels that we had never stepped into. Atsa certainly had never been to one and she had always aired her suspicions that the hotels probably did not boil the meat long enough. She would have been happy to know that her house was being used to prevent many of her relatives from eating food that had not been properly cooked.

SEVEN

Family History

Atsa's mother was from Rüsoma. When the war broke out, Atsa took her family out of Kohima and they lived for nearly two months in her ancestral village, which was considered a safer place than Kohima. Her father was a wealthy man and they were able to shelter three other families from Kohima. They shared their food with them and lasting friendships grew out of these actions. Fortunately, the war did not last long and after three months, DC Pawsey sent out orders for the people of Kohima village to return to their homes.

When Atsa was alive, her relatives would visit them bearing basketloads of vegetables—pumpkins, beans, maize, and mustard leaves in season. They were polite farmers from the village; some of them came wearing old clothes our grandparents had given them. The customary cotton *lohe* was draped over their upper body. No one travelled without a *lohe*. Even now the guests that came still used a *lohe*, especially if they were from the older generation.

I liked Azuo's recollections of her grandfather. 'Ntsa's father was a famous bone-setter. People from as far away as Dimapur came to him when they had broken a bone or twisted an ankle or any such injury. He was so skilled that if he set a broken bone, it healed within a couple of weeks, whereas a doctor would put it in plaster and wait for months for the bone to set. At the peak of his career, our grandfather moved to Kohima and operated from a small house in the Chotu Bosti area. In the village, people would pay him with vegetables or even live chickens. But in town, patients would give him money as payment, two rupees, five rupees, even ten rupees. He never asked for payment and didn't feel right about being paid in money. *This is a gift from Terhuomia*, he would say by way of refusing payment. But people were very grateful to be healed and forced gifts on him. They say that such people can bequeath their blessing to another member of the family. But we have not had anyone with his skills, not in your grandmother's generation or in mine, for that matter. It could very well reappear in your generation.'

'You mean Ato or I or Vilhou might become bone-setters?' I had asked incredulously.

'Maybe,' was Azuo's reply. 'It's not such a terrible thing to have a job that gives relief from pain to many people.'

'But isn't it something only for non-Christians? Azuo Zeü said that your grandfather used to mumble underneath his breath and talk to spirits before he attended to his patients.'

'Haha. He used to do that indeed. You've got a great memory. But he also helped a lot of people with what he knew, so it was not all bad.'

We never got to see Atsa's father and since there were no cameras at that time, we had no photos of him. The only photographs we had of Azuo's family were of our grandparents. Azuo and Azuo Zeü had identical framed photographs of their parents. We kept our copy in the sitting room, and Azuo Zeü kept hers on the bedside table along with other family photos.

Azuo said she and her older sister had not been very close when my father was alive. Not only was there a big age difference as Azuo Zeü was older by five years, the two of them had led their own lives, first with Azuo Zeü starting a family of her own, and Azuo immersed in her studies. They did get together for birthdays or Christmases which were all celebrated at our grandparents' house. But after they had both lost their spouses, not a day went by without the two sisters doing something or other together. Nowadays, it was activities like going grocery shopping in the week or eating dinners at our house. Azuo Zeü's husband outlived Apuo, but two years ago, he came down with a fever which was diagnosed as pneumonia and he died after a short illness. She was much changed now from the stern-faced aunt that I had known in my childhood. Vilhou's wife was a difficult person and Azuo Zeü felt that she had met her match in her daughter-in-law. She became quite subdued and preferred to spend time with her sister instead of wrangling with her daughter-in-law over insignificant issues. I thought she had become much more considerate of others as she got older. I certainly liked her better now.

She would often seek my advice on office matters: after her midwifery training, Azuo Zeü had had a long career as a senior midwife in the civil hospital. I helped her with her pension papers and she was very grateful for that. My mother had very clear memories of growing up with her siblings.

'The two of them, Zeü and Amo, were out of the house before I was grown. This was after Razou had died and I used to feel very lonely at times, coming home after school to an empty house. There were no siblings for me to play with and Ntsa would be busy in the garden, quite oblivious to how lonely a child could get on its own. When Zeü came home wearing her nursing uniform, how we all admired her. It was quite incredible that Zeü could have become a midwife, with all the knowledge that comes with it. She used big medical words that none of us understood and we were so proud of her. Already, there were a few Naga doctors during the war; at this time, they were all men of course. Then we heard that one young woman had been brave enough to enrol for MBBS. It was in 1952 that Khrielieü Kire became the first Naga lady doctor. How proud we were and how inspiring the news was. Not only were our girls becoming nurses, they were also becoming doctors! There would be no stopping them now! Dr Khrielieü had been about eight years senior to Zeü at school. Father told me I could try to follow in her footsteps, but I was very weak in Mathematics, so there was no possibility of me becoming anything in the medical profession.

Amo surprised everyone when he said he wanted to become a soldier. Ntsa and Npuotsa thought he would want to study further and were saving money for the day when he would leave the nest. When he passed his tenth, he announced that he was going to recruit in the army.

"We have never had a soldier in the family before," Ntsa had protested. But his mind was made up. He asked for their blessings saying he would join the army with or without their consent and wasn't it better to send him off with their blessings? They had to reluctantly agree, and on the day he was called up, Ntsa prayed a long prayer of protection over him. He promised to be careful and then he was gone, carrying his clothes and belongings in an army rucksack and running off to join his friends. We watched him go and when he caught up with his friends, he turned back to wave at us. When he did that, all of us cried because we realised that he might not return.

Many young Naga men were running off to join the British army in those days because the pay was good and no young man could resist getting a rifle to call his own. There are songs written about these men. They were composed by the women of their age-group talking about their failure to persuade their men-friends to stay. They tell how the parents of the young men had gone to the young women to ask them to persuade their male friends not to abandon the village by joining the army. The songs are about young men who would not give up their love of the soldier's life, undeterred by parental threats and unmoved by the soft words of their women friends.

Men like Amo truly believed that to be a soldier was a noble calling. On his rare visits home, he brought his rations and gave them to Ntsa. He had saved almost all his salary and brought it home to our parents.

"Did you starve yourself? This is too much money!" Ntsa had protested.

"Azuo, the army feeds us very well," he had smilingly replied. On his visits, the neighbourhood children would come running to the house calling out, "Amo! Amo!" They knew he would not forget to bring them sweets. He would laugh and go out to meet them with his hands full of candy and throw it in the air for them to scramble after. He made sure that every child got a sweet and if some were unlucky, he always had some in his pocket for them.

He was very young then, closing in on or just turned 17. Even after he recovered from his war wounds, he asked to rejoin his unit. But his officers would not let him do any heavy work, so he was given some small jobs in the office, and in any case the war was practically over by the time he was back on his feet. His doctors had told his officers that he was at risk of his life and was discouraged from rigorous work of any kind. After a few years, he was given an honourable mention for his devotion to duty, and citing his war wound, they released him from his duties and put him on a pension.

Some of Amo's friends who became soldiers around the same time as him never made it back. We heard they had died in Burma fighting the Japanese. Their bodies did not reach their families. That was a very sad thing for the family because our mourning customs are done around our dead, and in such circumstances, the family struggles to find healing and closure. In the years after the war, people were preoccupied with rebuilding their homes and their lives, and they were unable to give attention to these bereaved families. I feel sorry for them. They must have struggled alone without knowing what to do. Some soldiers who returned alive had missing limbs. They had to be rehabilitated in the hospital in

Shillong. In our village, there was a man with a leg missing. He had stepped on a mine. He was lucky to get away with his life. He used to live on a military pension for the disabled.

We grew up very quickly after the war. It was inevitable. We had seen too much. Before the war, no one had even seen an aeroplane. During the war, our skies were filled with all sorts of planes. Some would drop rations, some dropped leaflets, and some others bombed the areas where the Japanese were reported to be camping. We had no proper roads before the war; we only had the Imphal-Dimapur road which was quite narrow and was a one-way road. Numerous roads were built after the war: widening village paths, digging new routes and connecting them to the main highway between Imphal and Dimapur. At the time, many of our people could not imagine that there was such a big world beyond our hills. The war brought the outside world so much closer to us; in fact, it brought the world to us. And it brought home the reality of death to our young minds. There were many bodies of dead soldiers when we returned as the army had not been able to clear them all. People found dead Japanese soldiers in their fields in the village land areas. Ntsa used to tell us about a friend of theirs, Zeno, who was a midwife. We called her Ania because she was related to Npuotsa. Zeno buried many of the Japanese by herself. She was a very brave woman. She had already been working in the hospital before the war.'

EIGHT

The Town

Our tea cups stood on the low table, growing cold. We quickly finished our tea and Azuo continued with her story.

'Before the war, our headmaster Mr. Supplee used to listen to the radio a lot. It made us curious to listen to the news from outside. I bought a transistor radio with my first salary and your grandfather and I would listen to the news at night. Ntsa would complain that the noise bothered her. *Khonuo trazitor-u* was her name for my radio set. She took to going to the bedroom early if we brought out the radio. If she remained in the kitchen, she would sit through the news muttering that she couldn't get anyone to do anything when *that thing* was on.

In those days, if you went to people's houses in the evening after dinner, you would find the family sitting together, listening to the radio. It was the result of education and the very real fact that the war had opened up the world for us. We were curious about what was going on beyond our hills. Much of my knowledge about the outside world came via that little radio that we used to listen to every evening. That and the newspapers that came once a week. We would devour the newspapers when they finally arrived, making sure to read every page.

Many trees were planted by the government after the war. They planted trees at the Raj Bhavan area, which had the wartime name of "Garrison Hill". All the trees had been destroyed by mortar shelling and only the stumps were left. Workers removed the stumps and planted new saplings in their places. A lot of work was done on the war cemetery area, planting of flowers between the graves and making paths along each bed. Memorials were erected with a brief summary of the battle of Kohima and the fierce fighting before it was finally won. People often visited the war memorial, respectfully stopping at each plaque to read the inscriptions on it and wonder that such a major battle had been fought here on our lands just a few years ago.

There was something quite remarkable in the manner in which the flowers grew back. They sprouted along the little lanes between houses, and in every spot that had not been dug up or bulldozed over. The ground did not stay barren for long. The rains had set it off. Grass grew back over the barren patches, weeds took over, and small flowers blossomed amongst the weeds. When our people went to till their fields, they had to work harder because weeds had grown unhindered over the fields in the months where they had neglected to tend them. In fact, the weeds proved quite stubborn to get rid of since no one had taken a *dao* to them for months. Yet even in the fields, the flowers blossomed until ruined by the incessant rains.

When the rains retreated, golden yellow sunflowers covered the valley areas and the pink and white cosmos flowers could be seen everywhere. It was almost as though the flowers were blooming abundantly in an effort to hide what the war had done to the land.

The British had left for good in 1947 when DC Pawsey closed down his office and drove out of Kohima for the last time. It was the end of an era, in a manner of speaking. It was a strange feeling. Many of our people had not known any government other than the British. So, when they left our hills, many people felt orphaned, including grown people. You have to understand that these were the people who were born under British rule and had grown up in an environment that was supervised by rules and directives. Even though they had led fairly independent lives tilling their fields from dusk to dawn, they had become used to the presence of a government that took care of matters that were too big for them, such as the Japanese invasion. The village people were saying, "Our parents are leaving us." It was said with sadness and a sense of helplessness.'

It was difficult for Azuo to describe what followed after the British had left. But I knew from accounts of our people who lived through that period that they saw great political changes. It started when the British had mapped our territories and divided our lands between India and Burma, the new nations. Our leaders organised protests against this action and refused to join the Indian union. Even while the few educated Nagas felt that they had the right to fight for Naga sovereignty, the Indian government sent in armed police who began a reign of terror. They tried to crush the

movement for Naga sovereignty and started killing those who
opposed them. The Naga National Council was established
in 1946. Eventually the Naga National Council organised an
army unit and took up arms against the Indian government
because many people were being tortured in the interior
areas and whole villages were undergoing 'grouping' as part
of the Indian government's strategy to suppress the freedom
movement. The villagers were made to sit outside all day
without food or water. Old people and young children were
all included in that group, resulting in deaths from starvation
and beatings. Azuo had tears in her eyes when she tried to tell
me about the sufferings of the people.

'We were no longer safe in our own homes. At any time,
the army would barge in the door and search our homes. At
random moments, curfew would be announced for several
days. It was very dangerous to go out if there was a curfew on.
The soldiers shot anybody who ventured out at such times.
Civilians were killed in this period. It was so much worse for
those in the villages because the army conducted groupings
of the whole village for days and they could not go to their
fields. We heard that women were raped in these villages. So
many men joined the Naga army to fight against the Indian
government. So many of those men died; it was like a whole
generation of men disappeared because they were all killed,
one after the other.

In the town, we had some semblance of normal life and
people went to their fields or to schools and offices. But even
here, there were times when shootings would suddenly erupt
and we would run home as fast as we could. People whose
family members were in the Naga army were harassed by

the soldiers. They were sent to prison in a bid to make their relatives surrender. The American missionary family had been forced by the government to leave in 1949. Things got much worse after that.

Amongst our people, there was sympathy for the Naga Underground as the Indian government called them, but it was so dangerous to try and help them. They hid in the jungles and could visit their loved ones only at great risk to themselves. Their houses were under surveillance and the movements of their family members were closely monitored so that it was almost impossible for them to come back to the villages, even briefly. Life was so much worse than it was during the Japanese war. In those days, although bombs were falling all around us, we were never the target of the bombings. British and Indian soldiers came by the thousands but we never feared them; we knew they were there to protect our lands. But now people had grown to fear the sight of the Indian soldiers.

At the peak of the fighting, we had to close all schools indefinitely. Those families who could afford it sent their children to study in Assam and Shillong. Along with Ntsa and Npuotsa and Nzuo Zeü's family, we travelled to Shillong to live with a relative there. We were away for about three months. When the news reached us that things were better and we could return home, we took a taxi to Gauhati and caught a train from there to Dimapur. But when we reached Kohima, it was not much better than when we had left. There were even more soldiers in town. The army were still imposing curfews and spontaneous firing could occur in the middle of the night. It continued to be very risky to live in

Kohima. Yet we did not want to make another major move as we had done when we went to Shillong. Ntsa would call all of us into her bedroom for nightly prayers. She was so sure it was our nightly prayers that had protected the family in those years. At least our house was not under surveillance as some of our neighbours' houses were.

My friend Lydia's brother had joined the Naga army early on. Her poor mother would worry all the time as they could not get any news of him. From time to time, after months, a letter might come from him. But they never knew where he was as it was too dangerous. I don't think it was even a letter, but just a message to let them know he was still alive. 'That poor boy James,' Ntsa would say when she talked about him and prayed for him; she would conclude all her prayers with 'and Lord keep that poor boy James safe.' James was killed when his camp was ambushed by Indian soldiers. They couldn't bring his body home so they brought back his diary and his copy of the New Testament. His mother said these articles would be buried with her when she died. I think that was another reason why they moved to Dimapur; people move away from a place where they have known unbelievable loss.

We had shortages of food during the curfews: no prior notice was given before a curfew was declared. If people had not stocked food, they had to go without because it was too dangerous to go out of the house at the time. You couldn't even go to your neighbour's house and borrow an item you needed. We learned to stock the food items we didn't want to be without in an emergency. We kept extra rations in the cellar. At night, whenever possible, our family slept on the ground by pulling mattresses onto the floor. Npuotsa insisted on that as firing could happen at any time and it was possible for bullets to penetrate the tin walls and hurt people. It had happened to our neighbours.

There was no electricity then. People used kerosene lanterns after dusk. At night, in the absence of electricity, it would become pitch dark which was an advantage for the Naga Underground. They became adept at moving around under cover of darkness. In the 50s, they used to ambush Indian army convoys and shoot at patrolling parties and take away their weapons. If they were planning to attack an army convoy, they would send out warnings to civilians not to travel on those routes.

From time to time, the Naga Underground recruited young people into its fold. Nmi Amo was one of those who came onto their radar. He was still young and had army experience. But Ntsa firmly stopped him joining them. She reminded him of his injury and asked him if he wanted her dead before her time. Wasn't once enough? she asked. Amo promised her he would not do anything to make her worry on his account. He would be, of course, very upset when he heard of or saw the way our people were being treated by the government. We know he would have joined up if it had not been for Ntsa.'

At least Azuo's family were spared the anxiety of having a member in the Underground. Some men who were young fathers had left their wives and small children behind them, spurred on by their duty to their motherland. It was a nationalism that went very deep; it was difficult for men to stay away from the struggle. Even women joined the

Underground and fought alongside the men for many years. They had different reasons. Some women were there because their brothers or fathers had died at the hands of the Indian army. It was not easy for the Indian government to try to wipe out the movement.

The members had deep rooted cultural and religious reasons for fighting the war. The non-Christians believed that if they failed to avenge the killing of a family member, they would have failed in their obligation to the deceased member. Our culture was also our religion, so people were prepared to fight desperately or die trying. The fact that they were there to protect the land was never forgotten, but these other factors were also behind the growing ranks of the Naga Underground. It appealed to the Naga man's sense of nobility and that was partly why it was so hard to suppress. Men were ready to give their lives for this noble cause. Was it because it was so close to the Japanese war where they had witnessed men laying down their lives to defend Kohima against the invaders? It was difficult to say. Something in the souls of these men had been aroused and they fought tenaciously for many years and the war for Naga sovereignty became a long drawn out war.

NINE

Marrying in the Middle of War

The marvel of the period was that even as the war was being carried out all around them, in the townships people tried to live their lives as close to normal as was allowed. School was conducted when it was peaceful enough to have classes. Every now and then, the even tenor of life would be interrupted by a killing—sudden gunfire in encounters between the army and the Underground which sent people scampering for home and destroyed any semblance of normal life in an instant. But the next morning, the townspeople would pick up their lives and get back into the routine of daily life. That was the only way to survive. Marriages were conducted, newlyweds started families, and in the midst of all that my parents met and married.

'We had a small wedding, your father and I,' Azuo said in reply to my prompting. 'In 1959, there were not too many days that were peaceful. I think it was for that reason that we were even more determined to marry and spend our lives together. We did not make an invitation card. Our two sets of parents went around and invited all their relatives: that included cousins on both sides. Somehow Ntsa was able to send word to her people in Rüsoma. It would have been very rude not to invite them to the last wedding in the family. On your father's side, they invited their clan members, taking care not to leave out anyone. Two days before the wedding, the men from your father's clan came to Npuotsa's house with a cow and a pig, the animals that were to be slaughtered for the wedding feast. Npuotsa had made sure that there were some elderly male relatives to receive the group. The oldest among them gave a speech thanking your father's people and receiving the animals on our behalf.

On that same day, there were some women in our house pounding paddy to be cooked on the wedding day. The two groups exchanged light-hearted jokes after the ceremony of handing over the animals was done. The women told the men to come for the wedding having sharpened their teeth to eat meat.

The men returned the next day and put up a tarpaulin shelter for the wedding guests. Some of the girls from my side arrived and busied themselves cutting up coloured paper to hang across the bamboo poles over which the tarpaulin was spread.

On my wedding day, I wore a *lora mhoushü* waist-cloth, and a white long-sleeved blouse made of velvet. That was what brides usually wore in our days. I didn't have a veil. We still had many non-Christian relatives and they wouldn't understand the significance of a veil, so I chose to forego it. Nzuo Zeü made a bouquet of small pink roses for me to carry. Npuo wore a dark suit and everyone remarked how handsome he looked. We took photographs before and after the ceremony. The pastor had agreed to come to the house and solemnise the marriage. It saved us a long walk to church and a long walk back home where the feast had been prepared. After the ceremony we hurried through the rest of the formalities as we knew people would become anxious to get home before any trouble started. That was how life was in the late 50s. One never knew when and where firing would start. The war was no respecter of persons. People had to take their chances and do what they wanted to do, and hope for the best.'

We still kept their wedding album carefully in the sitting room. Some of the photographs were blurry, but the rest were very clear pictures of the two of them and the guests. In three of the photographs, Azuo was smiling happily at the camera in her *lora mhoushü*, a white cloth with black stripes on the border and geometrical patterns scattered over the cloth. My very young father had a hairstyle I had never seen on him. His oiled hair was brushed back in the fashion of the day and he was proudly smiling at the camera. My father was the only man in the photographs who wore a tie. None of the other men did although they were all dressed in their best. Many of them had a *lohe* slung over their shoulders. A few wore the black body-cloth and it covered their chests completely so that you could not see the red and green stripes that made up the border. This was the traditional body-cloth for all occasions. At festivals they teamed it with the white *lora mhoushü* and the combination of the two cloths looked well. On its own, the *lohe* was sombre and uninspiring although Azuo said it was a very dignified piece of clothing.

The women in the photographs could be divided into
two groups. The ones who had been to school wore dresses
and skirts and looked almost coquettish as they posed for
the camera. One woman wore a short coat and sported a
beret on her curly head. Almost all the women had identical
hairstyles, tight curls in a side part, secured with a bow or hair
band. The ones who sported long hair had their hair in plaits
wound in front and tied at the back. Those who had carried
handbags made sure to display them in front. The women
were thronged around my mother in the photographs.
Giggling and waving. Looking carefree as though they had
no troubles at all.

The other group of women were dressed in the traditional
waist-cloth and body-cloth. They stood at a distance and
looked solemn. They almost seemed to be not part of the
wedding celebration at all. When the photographer pointed
the camera at them, some of them quickly pulled up their
cloths so that their faces were half covered. Those who
were smiling looked nervous, and those who did not want
to be photographed had turned their faces away. Many
of our people in the villages were reluctant to have their
pictures taken. To see their images in a photograph greatly
embarrassed them, and their friends would tease them
about the way they were smiling, or not smiling, and make
comments about their hair or teeth and so on.

There was one group photo, as it was called, taken of all
the wedding guests standing in rows behind the nuptial pair.
It was so small that it was not possible to make out anyone.
But Azuo would point out different people and tell us, 'That
is Nzuo Lydia, and that is her cousin sister, Jasino. That man

at the back is Nzuo Zeü's husband, and that woman beside him is his mother, not Nzuo Zeü. Oh, there is Nmi Amo with his friends—I wonder what they were laughing at. That man in the hat is your father's uncle.' I would peer and peer at the little people in the picture and wonder how Azuo could make out their features and be able to identify almost all of them. I couldn't. In fact, when I found a magnifying glass, I tried looking at the small black and white print through the glass. It enlarged the picture but to my disappointment, the people were indistinguishable. Only the man in the hat stood out a bit because he was the only one wearing a hat. The figure standing to the side holding a Bible was the pastor. Azuo could not possibly have noticed that Ami Amo and his friends were laughing, except for the fact that he was bending over. Again, to me he was just another small black dot amongst the many other black dots.

'We weren't the only ones to get married in that year. In fact, there were five weddings in the same year. Lydia had married three years before us and it was very nice of her to come to my wedding with her husband and mother. Npuo and I went to live in his father's house in the first month. Luckily, we soon found a house close to the school that we could rent, so we moved there. Ntsa worried so much that we might be harassed by burglars and we eventually built a house very close to them. Truth be told, we felt we were quite safe near the school, except for the times the army came to check our house for the Underground. Npuo did not believe we were going about fighting for freedom the right way. He being such a peaceful man, no one could persuade him to join the Underground. I had peace of mind about that as I had seen how hard it was for the wives left behind to look after young children. At the same time, people like us feel guilty and see ourselves as not contributing anything to the struggle.

I sometimes visited these women and brought them food or clothes; on their part, they never begged for food or anything. Our ways are so rigid. People would rather die than beg. It was up to the individual to be observant and help when he saw the need.

Npuo and I continued to teach at the Government High School and in the third year I had to take maternity leave when you were born.'

Part Two

TEN

I Am Born

I was born on the 6th of January, 1961. My mother told me it was a very cold morning. There was frost on the ground and she shivered uncontrollably when the midwife was helping her with the birthing. Atsa Bonuo had made a coal fire in the *chullah* to keep the room warm. They put woollen socks on Azuo's feet and kept her covered with a blanket under which the midwife used a torch to see that all was going as it should.

Fortunately, the labour did not last too long and soon Apuo could be told he had a daughter. I don't remember him carrying me and looking down at my mother with tears in his eyes. I don't remember the two of them holding each other with me in the middle getting squashed. I don't remember crying out for milk, or water, or even just dear life at that point. But according to my mother, I gave a loud cry and the midwife quickly took me from my parents and cleaned me up. Atsa Bonuo named me Kevinuo.

My childhood was narrated to me by my father and my mother and my grandparents. I did not have any memory of my childhood until I turned three. My adventures with cats and dogs around the house and my attempts at crawling, and eventually walking and talking, were all related to me by the grown-ups in my life.

'You were a very calm baby,' Atsa Bonuo would tell me, 'but Npuotsa spoiled you. He carried you around all the time. Even when you could walk quite well by yourself, you would ask to be carried.'

'You always fell asleep if I carried you and sang to you,' Apuotsa would remind me, 'That's why I carried you so much.'

Apuotsa's sister, Atsa Nisoü, used to scold, 'You are all spoiling this child. Let her walk, she can walk, can't she? Or is she still crawling?'

Atsa Nisoü was a lean-faced woman; her house was in the village. She visited Atsa at least once a week and since we spent so much time at Atsa's house, she would supervise my upbringing.

'Look at her legs, she needs oiling every morning. There's no other cure for bow legs like that!'

As I grew bigger, Atsa Nisoü became a prominent part of my childhood. She brought vegetables on her visits to my grandparents, and she would throw out little titbits of instructions on how to raise a child, especially if it was female. Atsa Bonuo and Apuotsa lived on the land where the village tapered off to join the town boundary. It was technically under the jurisdiction of the village, and if a *genna*-day, when any work was considered taboo, was being observed, they would abide by it too. In the early days, the area where they had built their house was said to have been the roaming ground of a warrior spirit. When he was sighted, he would be seen wearing the traditional garb of a warrior and carrying a spear. He was gigantic in size. Many people had reported sighting him especially during the evening hours; he often rushed towards them aggressively.

Atsa Bonuo had no problem with these sightings. *Jesus will protect you*, she would say to any grandchild who expressed fear of the warrior spirit. But we were not so sure what Jesus could do against a spirit who had established his reputation so firmly in the area. Atsa Nisoü was not a Christian. She reported meeting the spirit many times. She said that the last time she met him, the encounter frightened her so much that she got very angry and she spat at him and cursed him. 'He ran off when I spat at him. Even spirits know what an ignominy it is to be spat on. And they should know because they themselves gave us all the customs we follow today!' I didn't know anyone else who had seen the warrior spirit so many times. When I was older I asked her,

'Atsa, how many times have you seen Keshüdi?' That was his name in Tenyidie.

'Child, I have seen him countless times. I can't remember. I think I have seen him every time I have been here to visit your grandparents. Maybe he doesn't like that I come here so often,' she laughed.

'Why is that?' I asked with the innocence of a child.

'Well, I don't know if you have noticed, but I am not a Christian like your grandparents are. So maybe he is worried I will start going to church like your family if I come here too often!' she laughed at the idea.

I was five years old then and did not fully understand what

she meant. She made it sound like the spirit and she were acquaintances, in a way. It was a very odd thought.

'Oh, don't think about it, my girl. You see, spirits are scared of Christians; they cannot approach them because it can end badly for the spirits. They prefer to make contact with us non-Christians, and that is why they frighten us and try to prevent us going over to the Christian side. When you are older I will tell you more.' With that promise she stopped talking about her spirit encounters.

When Atsa Nisoü came to visit, the two of them dug Atsa Bonuo's garden and sowed seeds at different seasons of the year. On the days that Azuo and Apuo went to work, I was left with Atsa Bonuo. We ate lunch only when they stopped to rest from digging the hard soil and knocking the clods of earth into smaller pieces with the backs of their spades. Sometimes Atsa Nisoü took a hammer and hammered at the earth with all her strength. 'There, take that!' she would shout, as though she were using the hammer like a weapon. It always made Atsa Bonuo laugh.

When they were finished, they came inside Atsa Bonuo's dark kitchen with Atsa Nisoü exclaiming,

'*Hou!* It's so dark in here I'm afraid I will knock something over!'

'No, you won't,' Atsa Bonuo replied, 'Just wait there by the door and let your eyes adjust.' That was a trick I learned early to be able to see inside Atsa Bonuo's kitchen. It seldom failed to work. But if it was still dark, you simply had to be more patient and wait in the corner until it cleared.

'Wash your hands and I'll serve you some food,' Atsa Bonuo instructed us. She herself had finished cleaning her hands by the time her companion had groped her way to a chair. Atsa Bonuo served me food in my little enamel bowl. It had a blue and red flower print and a dark blue border. I had a little blue spoon to go with it.

'Can I get a spoon just like yours?' Atsa Nisoü began to tease me. 'I really want to eat my food with a spoon just like yours.'

'We haven't got another blue spoon, Atsa.'

'Could I borrow it just for today?' she kept on teasing me. Atsa Bonuo regularly made dal and a chutney for the grown-ups. I got a boiled egg every day. Sometimes she would make egg omelette for all of us. I liked that very much.

'Kevinuo, eat up,' she urged me. 'Eat everything on your plate. We are so lucky we have food. There are children in India who don't get any food.'

'What about rice and dal?' I had asked once.

'Not even that,' Atsa Bonuo had stated very firmly.

As I ate, I would feel sorry for the children in India and wonder if I could send them my food on some of the days. But when I asked Apuotsa about it, he said India was very far from us, and that there were many children who needed food, not just one or two. Luckily, I had a good appetite and rarely needed threats to finish eating my food.

ELEVEN

Ato Is Born

At home, Azuo had been unwell for some weeks. One night when I was asleep, my brother came into the world. Next morning, I heard him crying in my parents' room. 'Come and meet your brother,' Azuo called me over. For some inexplicable reason I felt very shy. Apuo pulled me over to the bed and held me up so I could see him. He was red all over and had a small chest. He cried a lot.

'You have to give him a name. He hasn't got one. Can you do that, Kevinuo?' Apuo asked. I swallowed hard. I had never given anyone a name before, not even a dog or a cat.

'He is your brother. You must give him a name,' he insisted.

'I'll ask Apuotsa or Atsa,' I countered.

'No, that is cheating. If you ask someone else for help, it will be their name. You have to do it on your own.' Apuo looked very serious as he said this. Then he smiled and said, 'Don't worry, I'll help you.'

All morning the two of us went around thinking up suitable names. Finally, I came up with Ato.

'Oh, what a sweet name,' Azuo said when we told her. 'We will call him Ato, of course.' My brother had another name in the school register. *Vingutuo*. But at home and amongst his friends, everyone called him Ato.

Atsa Bonuo and Apuotsa and Atsa Nisoü were very happy at the birth. In the days after Ato's birth, I stayed at home because Azuo was confined to bed, and she said she needed me to help her. I felt proud when she said that and I stayed by her side as much as possible instead of running out to play.

Ato cried often. When that happened, Azuo nursed him, or bathed him, or checked that he had not wetted himself. He didn't stay small very long. In the months that followed he cried much less and he began to grow bigger. When Azuo bathed him, I would help her by running off to get a cloth she needed or cotton wool for her to clean his ears. Although it was nice to stay at Atsa Bonuo's house, it was so much nicer to stay at home and help Azuo with her new baby.

Atsa Bonuo called to ask if I should come stay with her so that I could be out of the way, but Azuo said I was her little helper and that she needed me around. Ato did not like the dark. He cried when he was left alone in a room. I wondered if it could be that he was not a Christian and could see frightening spirits in the room. If what Atsa Nisoü said was true, the spirits could be trying to get close to him before he became a Christian. I resolved to watch over him as much as I could.

'You can carry him when he is a bit older. Not now,' Azuo said when I wanted to carry him on my back. But she would lift him up and place him on my back and let me feel his weight. He was very heavy though he didn't look it.

I wanted so much to carry him that I was given a puppy to carry instead.

Ato was crawling at eight months. He got into all kinds of awkward spaces, like under the kitchen table, or between the sofa and the wall, and he would stay there crying until someone helped him out. He was a very active child, and in no time, he was walking unsteadily using chairs and low tables as hand-holds.

Ato's first word was *Ovi*, his name for me. He must have heard everyone calling me Kevinuo or Kevi, and somehow learned to produce something close to it.

'What's he saying? What does it mean?' Azuo asked the first time he called out the new word. I listened but did not understand either.

'Ato, what are you trying to say? Do you want some milk? Do you want your toy car?' I asked him question after question. He came close to me and poked me and said it again, 'Ovi!' We all burst out laughing when we realised he was saying my name. The next week he could call out *Zho* for Azuo and *Po* for Apuo. He had shortened versions of people's names; Atsa became *Cha* and Apuotsa became *Pocha*. Even when he grew older and began to start at school, Ato's habit of shortening words made it difficult for the teachers to understand him. They struggled until they figured out that he was so used to shortening long words that he couldn't be bothered to use the full form. It was only after much training that they were able to get him to pronounce the words in their full forms. For instance, he would say *fant* instead of elephant, *raff* instead of giraffe, and *liter* in place of alligator. He was five years old at that time and was perfectly capable of enunciating words properly. He still continued to call me Ovi until he was teased by his friends about it when he was eight. From then on, he began to haltingly call me by my full name.

We both attended the Baptist English School which everyone called BE School for short. At that time there was another school newly opened by Beilieü Shüya called the National School. Both schools were close to us as we lived up the road in the house my parents had built close to my grandparents. By the time Ato joined school I was in the third grade. On the first day of school he was quite excited to join me. But when he saw his classmates crying and clinging to their parents, he looked unsure for some moments and then he too began to cry. He stayed away for the next two days before he could be persuaded to return. It was a good thing he had stayed away because in that time, his mates had settled down and were not crying any more. In the first weeks, if the teachers found Ato whining to go home, they would summon me from class and I would have to calm him down, promising we would go home soon. It was embarrassing to be called out of class in that manner as everyone would look when you came back to class. My best friend Beinuo gave my hand a squeeze when I was called out the first time. She had had to do this for her younger sister in the previous year.

Thankfully, Ato settled down and our routine of going to school at 7.30 in the morning became a regular thing. When we walked to school we met our friends along the road, and we would all walk together in a big group. Azuo would come with us until the school gate. Parents were allowed inside the classroom for the new children. But Azuo wanted Ato to become more independent so she always waved goodbye at the gate and waited and waited until we were inside our classrooms. He made friends with two of the boys who sat with him. One was an Ao boy called Chuba and the other boy was a Nepali boy called Nobin. Ato came home another day saying he wanted to have a box of crayons exactly like Chuba's.

TWELVE

Vilhoulie

In our house we had electricity and we didn't have to do our homework using kerosene lamps. We were very fortunate. The year I was born only a few houses, such as the Deputy Commissioner's, had electricity. When statehood came two years later, electrification was installed in all the main towns in the state. Even in Atsa Bonuo's house, Apuo persuaded them to install electricity, and they did after some years, but they still used their kerosene lamps in the kitchen. If we ate dinner at their house, Atsa Bonuo would have the kerosene lamps lit alongside the electric bulb.

'My goodness, Ania, it is almost as bright as day in here,' Apuo had teased her the first time because he knew how dark her kitchen was in the daytime. To hear Apuo exclaim Atsa Bonuo's kitchen was bright as day was highly amusing for the rest of us.

'At least she allowed me to put a bulb in here,' Apuotsa had told us.

In the days before electricity, Azuo and Azuo Zeü used a coal iron for all their clothes including our school uniforms. Most people used only that and it worked as well as the electric iron, which came to the shops only in the late 60s.

Electrification eventually reached the rural areas after some years. It was such a great event for our people.

'Did you hear that they are now using electricity in Rükhroma? Can you just imagine that!' Atsa Bonuo exclaimed excitedly when we visited her. She could not imagine her home village could become so modernised. But it was a time when the whole state was seeing improved standards of living. The Nagaland State Transport buses began services between the main towns. With the introduction of bus services, people began to travel more frequently. Kohima was growing rapidly; forested areas were cut down to make room for new houses. More people flocked to the capital town to work or start a business. New shops opened beside the already existing old shops and the town area began to extend beyond the TCP gate.

As a child, something I thoroughly enjoyed was to accompany Azuo to the vegetable market in the heart of the town. Next to the vegetable sellers, men of Kohima village had set up meat stalls and they ran a very good business of selling freshly butchered meat. The village women sat in the open and sold their wares, fresh and dried herbs, pumpkins, beans, and vegetables in season. Whenever they saw us, the meat sellers would call out to us to buy their meat. They often had big foaming mugs of rice brew at their side from which they would drink from time to time. I found everything interesting and on one of our trips, a meat seller called out,

'Aneinuo, come here and drink from my mug, come.' I was about to happily run to him and accept his offer when Azuo took my hand and held it fiercely so I could not move.

Back at home I asked her why I was not allowed to drink from the man's brew mug. The foaming white fluid looked like milk to me and I imagined it would taste like milk. Azuo explained that it was not milk but rice-brew, that I would get drunk and then how would she carry such a big girl like me home? And worse, if I got drunk people would talk about us, the whole town would. After that, I avoided going past the meat sellers and attracting their attention. I would hide behind my mother until she finished her purchases and then we would go straight home.

Besides the meat sellers I had not seen many men drinking when I was growing up. In the village, men would sit all day with a mug of brew but it was not polite to get drunk. However, we had our neighbourhood drunk who would come home late at night shouting all the way up the road. He carried a walking stick which he waved about, and everyone got out of his way if they saw him coming. Ato and I always ran to peek from behind the curtain when we heard him coming. He rarely went home alone; one or two men usually accompanied him from the drinking house and made sure he reached his house safely. His wife had died many years ago and people said that was the reason for his drinking. He was a frightful sight when he came waving his stick and shouting curses whenever they escorted him home. Luckily for us he lived a few houses away, so we would wait until the cursing noises went past our house and then we would come out cautiously and peer in the direction in which he had gone.

He had once hit a young man with his stick, so most people avoided him when he was in that condition. Ato and I were mortally afraid of him, yet we were greatly fascinated by the sight of his drunkenness. So long as we were safe inside our home we wanted to watch the spectacle of a grown man drunkenly abusing everyone in sight. But if we were to meet him on our way home, we would both run as fast as our feet would carry us.

Apuo did not drink. Ami Amo had never been interested in alcohol though he had friends who liked to get drunk once in a while. What was it about drink that made grown men behave in such a disgraceful manner? I tried hard to understand that. They didn't seem to be aware that everyone was laughing at them, and they would either try to crack jokes or get angry and threaten to hit people. If we saw them the next day, they would shuffle past shamefaced, very different from the loud-mouths of the night before. Ato and I laughed at their antics but I also thought it was sad to see grown men behave like that. If he were my father I would not like people to see him like that.

When we were in the fifth grade, Beinuo and I were walking home from school when we saw our neighbour coming up the street on his own. He was very drunk and waving his stick. When he caught sight of the two of us, he raised his stick and began to give chase. We both screamed and ran as fast as we could. There was no one on the street at that hour. We ran up the hill to the first house, Azuo Zeü's, still screaming.

'What is happening?!' Azuo Zeü came to the door, took a look at us, and at our neighbour weaving his way up the slope.

She shouted, 'Get indoors now!' Then she stood with her hands on her hips and waited for him to reach her front yard.

'Vilhoulie, aren't you ashamed? Picking on children and frightening them out of their wits? Have you nothing better to do? Get home and stay home else I will report you to the police and you will have to spend the night in the lockup. It's only what you deserve, making the street dangerous for decent folk!' We heard every word from the house. Beinuo and I were holding each other's hands tightly. She was giving him the scolding of his life and we were so worried that he would try and hit her with his stick, but to our surprise, he stood there with his stick hanging down, saying sorry over and over again.

Azuo Zeü calmed down and accepted his sorrys. She even asked him if he wanted a cup of tea! He was too ashamed to say yes and went home.

'He's not a bad man, but he doesn't know how to deal with his problems and keeps using drink to forget them,' she said when he had gone. Not a bad man? We couldn't agree with her but we dared not tell her that.

'Next time, check if he is coming up the road and if he is, best to wait till he's gone,' she advised. Beinuo and I thanked her and left for our homes. Once at home, I told Azuo about it and said how scared we had been. She comforted me but said that we would have to be very careful.

'Don't leave the school on your own. As far as possible come with a big group. Be alert all the time. Don't hesitate to run if you feel frightened of anyone.' After that scare, Beinuo and I took to waiting until the teachers were ready to leave and we would follow close behind them.

Vilhoulie had no children. He had no family that we knew of. To us, he had always been a crazy old drunk man. None of the roles of husband, father or brother and son fitted him.

'He has been drinking for more than thirty years,' Azuo explained. 'When his wife was alive, he was a different man altogether. The two of them used to go to church every Sunday and he sang in the men's choir because he had a very good voice. Even when she became pregnant with their first child, he used to attend choir practice regularly. But when she died delivering a stillborn baby, he was very depressed and took to drink some months later. He has never been the same. He has lost people's sympathies by continuing to drink because when he is drunk he is such a terror with that stick of his.'

'Can't the police arrest him?' I asked. I felt that keeping him in prison would be the best solution.

'He has been in the lock-up several times, but they can't keep him in prison simply on account of his drinking,' Mother explained. 'Prison is for criminals, not social nuisances.'

Vilhoulie was an old man now and drink made him look older and more disagreeable than before. He came home drunk every evening. A couple of times he had surprised everyone when, instead of his customary cursing, he came up the road singing an old hymn quite clearly. After a while he became aware that people were listening and he got angry and shouted, 'That's the way to sing, you fools! Open your mouths and let the melody get out!' Having said that, he angrily sang the rest of the verse home and shut his front door with a bang.

Vilhoulie was not the only alcoholic who was around in our childhood. He just happened to be the most terrifying one. There were a few other men who drank rice-brew in the drinking houses in town. But they would go home quietly without raising the kind of ruckus that Vilhoulie was capable of. Brawls did happen but not frequently. If two men were brawling, it was the custom that other men would quickly come and pull them apart and escort each man home. If the men met when they were sober they would apologise to each other and put it behind them. That was what we knew of drunkenness in our childhood. All that began to change after some years. The political environment continued to contribute tension and uncertainty. The government came down harshly on men who would not surrender and 'join the mainstream,' as they called it. Frustration drove even more men to drink and alcohol abuse soon became a visible social problem.

THIRTEEN

Beinuo and Billy Graham

Beinuo and I were still classmates when we started High School. We had both cleared the sixth grade and gone on to the seventh. Apuo had died a few months before my final examinations, and all of us had somehow come through with our own scars. At school, my eyes would sometimes unexpectedly fill with tears, and I had trouble concentrating on my school work. The two of us moved to the back bench to avoid being asked questions all the time by the teachers. Once, the Mathematics teacher asked me a particularly tough question which I could not answer. I burst into tears. Beinuo pressed my hand and quickly passed me her handkerchief. I couldn't tell my mother what had happened when I got home because she was grieving over Apuo's death in her own way. She had become very distant and we always found ourselves tip-toeing around her, trying to avoid upsetting her.

I had somehow concluded that I had to act like an adult and had disappointed myself badly by breaking down in the classroom. The next day I feigned sickness and managed to avoid going to school for two days. I was not worried that my mother would discover my deceit. The only person who I feared would find me out was Azuo Zeü. She kept an eagle eye on me, checking that I had done my homework and inspecting my assignment papers, and commenting that I needed to work harder if I wanted to pass and go on to the eighth grade. It was not that I didn't care about my studies. I was fully aware of their importance, but what I really missed in my life was having an adult who could tell me how to cope with losing a father. If Ami Amo had been around maybe I could have asked him. Oh yes, I would have asked him and he would have helped me understand it all. But Ami Amo had died four years before my father. And it would be quite useless asking Azuo Zeü, who I suspected, would come down hard on any signs of weakness. At least I could tell Beinuo how I felt and she could understand since she had also lost her mother some years ago.

That was the thing I liked so much about Beinuo. She understood what it was to lose someone you dearly loved. She wouldn't say much; neither of us knew how to do that. It was enough to have a close friend to share your sadness with. Beinuo's home situation was much worse than mine. While I had an absentee mother, she had a new mother because her father had remarried. Her stepmother was pregnant with her second child and expected Beinuo to do all the housework when she came home from school. Some days she had no time to do her homework and got punished for it at school. It really worried me when she began to talk about quitting school. Luckily her father strongly opposed that idea. 'Education alone can give you a better life,' he told her.

He began to send her to tuition in the morning hours so she could improve her marks. It made a big difference and she was soon doing very well and talking about going to college when we passed our tenth. That was our big dream—to pass our matriculation exams and go to college.

In the new year, Beinuo and I started High School. We were still considered juniors by the classes above us, but we felt older and more mature than the students in the sixth. There was a lot of excitement afoot because all the Kohima churches were coming together to host the Billy Graham crusade. The organisers came to our school to tell us about the crusade and what a great event it was going to be. They said that we could volunteer as scouts and guides and help them with the work. However, they also said that only senior students could register as volunteers so we were not eligible. Nevertheless, it was exciting enough to witness all that was going on around us. In no time, cafes had sprung up selling tea and home-made cookies to raise funds for the crusade. The women at church began to take active part in fundraising. All this was very new to us. In her kitchen, Atsa Bonuo had a special basket where she put aside some rice for the church every month. That was about all that we knew of fundraising for the church.

Azuo and Azuo Zeü were requested to help in the church. As a matter of fact, they both became very busy with all the extra church activities and this had a positive effect on my mother. It triggered something in her that helped her to come out of her deep depression after Apuo's death. It was like she had suddenly remembered she had children to care for, and in addition, a church that needed her contribution. The two of them would work all day but in the evening, Azuo began to go over my school work. This became a regular part of our evenings. Ato was still in the third standard and his homework was quickly finished with some help from me. I was the one who had to stay up late struggling with History lessons, Geography maps, and Mathematical sums. Azuo went through all the subjects with me and insisted I work more diligently. Sometimes I felt resentful when she said that and wanted to ask where she had been in the past year when I had been struggling alone. But it was not something a child could say to a parent. I'd done poorly in Science and so she arranged tuitions for me. Now I had to work harder than ever because Azuo's teaching background made her a hard taskmaster.

However, at the end of all that, my teacher commented that my work had improved considerably. It didn't make Azuo ease off on me. She said that it wasn't enough that the teacher was pleased; I had to try to get into the top positions in the class. She gave me a rigorous study routine to follow. In spite of all that, I have continued to thank the Billy Graham crusade for bringing my mother back to life.

It meant, of course, that there were restrictions on my movements and activities. Now I could not go off to Beinuo's house as often as I liked. Still it was so much better than having to watch my mother sitting listlessly in her chair, totally unconcerned about what went on around her. I didn't think Azuo would ever go back to that existence from now on. The rest of the year was swallowed up in a maelstrom of activity as the crusade drew near and the whole town geared up to participate in the great event.

The Billy Graham crusade became a historical marker for our people. I have heard men giving their testimonies in church that they had stopped drinking when Billy Graham came to Kohima. One of the men, named Lhouvitso, used to say,

> I came to Jesus Christ in the year 1972. Before that, I was the worst of sinners. After work I would go straight to the drinking house and sit there with a mug of brew amongst my mates, enacting anecdotes and having a jolly time. I wouldn't go home until my wife came to shout at me, and at all the others in the drinking house as well. But I didn't care. I loved to drink. Then one evening, two men came looking for me in the drinking house. We offered them drink, but they refused and they said they had come to tell us about Jesus. We replied that we knew all about that, but they did not leave. They said the Christians in Kohima were going to arrange a Billy Graham crusade and they invited us to help them host the crusade. I had heard of Billy Graham, of course, and was very surprised that he was coming to our town. I was even more surprised that they needed my help to arrange things! It made me think, what if I give up all this and become a Christian? It might be worth it if the rest of them are as polite and friendly as these two. It made me want to hear more about Jesus and find out what I had missed. I took my last drink that evening and have not regretted it since. The church baptised me and I became a member just before the crusade.

The men who had been former alcoholics were quite open about their past and had no inhibitions about giving their testimonies. They took on duties like ushering or reading the scriptures at services and even joined the men's choir. However, it was not the same for the women who used to run drinking houses. Those who gave up the business and came to church were welcomed by the members, but they struggled with their lack of self-worth. They would speak disparagingly about themselves. They would make sure others knew that they had been brew sellers before becoming Christians and that they felt unworthy and undeserving to be church members. A phrase they liked to use was, '*we sü tuo rei tuo kemo kemhie,*' which meant, 'My presence has no significance for anyone.' This extreme humility and self-condemnation continuously emerged every time they realised they had been given a chance to be part of respectable society again. They would attend every church service, but always stay on the edges, overwhelmed by a sense of unworthiness each time they were invited to participate.

Christmas came round but people had already used up so much energy on the crusade. It was a quiet Christmas and Ato spent all his money on firecrackers. Our church had a feast as usual, and the children came wearing new clothes and shoes. But there was something perfunctory about it all, like a ritual we were about to repeat all over again. All of a sudden, I felt sad and could not comprehend why. It was different from the sadness I felt at my father's passing away. I had been dealing with that in a much better way, not crying so much, not brooding as I had last year. This sadness was different. I felt that the magic had gone out of this year's Christmas; almost as if we had grown out of it and I didn't like it. I wondered if this was how it was when you became an adult.

But when we had a get-together before New Year's Eve, things were much better. I looked forward to the celebrations and was not disappointed. Beinuo and I volunteered to go herb gathering with our seniors in the Pulie Badze area. We were instructed to wear good, warm clothes as it was quite cold in the mountains. Early the next morning, we boarded a bus which drove us past the Science College and stopped at the foot of the mountain. We clambered off the bus excitedly and lined up to wait for our guides.

'We'll start climbing slowly. Don't wander off on your own. We will stop at a place where there are many herbs, pluck all we need, and return. Don't eat your lunch packs here as we will do that on our return trip.' Beinuo and I followed the others up the steep hillside and we wondered how we would find a foothold if we saw some herbs in these parts. After the steep climb, our guides brought us to a clearing where we could see herbs growing up the slopes.

'Start gathering here. Try not to uproot the plants,' they warned us. 'No, not like that, take the top leaves and leave the rest of the plant. That way it'll sprout back in a few weeks.' We needed no more urging; we filled our baskets with the tender leaves.

One of the senior girls showed us a red-stemmed leaf that was sour and could be used in making broth with dried meat. It was good for neutralising fat, she added. We filled our baskets within an hour. When we returned to the base of the mountain, everyone was ravenous. We shared the food we had brought and went home feeling proud of the day's labour. It was a good way to celebrate the New Year. This was the first time we had been included in the herb-gathering by our seniors, and we were elated about that. It would be our first time celebrating New Year like grownups. Beinuo had turned twelve and I had my birthday coming up in a week. We wanted to show that we could take our responsibilities seriously.

FOURTEEN

How to be a Respectable Woman

When school reopened, and we were in the first month of classes, one of the senior girls was expelled. The teachers said she was pregnant and no one knew until it was almost too late. She was eighteen, much older than the other girls. She should have finished High School but had failed twice. After she left, the headmistress marched all the girls from our class to the assembly room and lectured us on the evils of getting pregnant before marriage. We were quite terrified to hear what would happen to girls who did that. They would never find husbands; they would be expelled from church and school; no one would consider them respectable anymore. The senior girl who got pregnant was now confined to her house and forbidden from meeting anyone. She would have no chance of finishing her education even after having the baby. It was a horrible fate.

After she gave birth, we sometimes saw her with her child; she would return our greetings but always hurry away without giving us the opportunity to ask more about her life.

How did she take care of the child? I wondered. Where did she get money for food and clothes for both of them? I had to ask Azuo and Azuo Zeü these questions.

'Hush, Kevinuo, don't be so curious! Do you want to end up like her?' Azuo Zeü scolded me. Azuo simply said, 'Where would she get money from? She has become a burden to her poor parents who have to find food for the extra mouth. God forbid that any of you go that way!'

There was a lot of talk when she left school but a couple of months later something terrible happened to stop all talk on that subject. Life in town had continued to witness different happenings, some of them good, some much worse than what had happened to the senior girl. One evening, the Ruby cinema hall was ripped apart by a bomb that killed a number of people and crippled others who'd been in the hall. No one knew who was responsible and the government blamed the Underground. But the tragedy was immense and it made everyone forget the gossip around the senior girl. The bombing created great panic amongst the townspeople. Some boys feared dead were found hiding in their homes, and others who were not so lucky lost their limbs. It was a major disaster and at the site, people were quite paralysed by the great shock. But after the initial confusion, they quickly swung into action, helping to get the victims to hospital and providing care for the traumatised cinemagoers.

The families that lost their sons were inconsolable. In our lifetime it was one of the worst local tragedies. At least Ato, at eight years, was too young to have been part of it. There were many young boys in their teens who were in the habit of going to the cinema on their own. After the bombing, parents became very strict with their children. They were no longer allowed to go out after 5 pm. The parental strictures seemed a bit lame since the Ruby Cinema hall had been so damaged by the bomb blast that it had to close down completely.

However, it had given the townspeople a rude reminder that the conflict between the Naga Underground and the government of India was still highly volatile and begging a solution. The ceasefire of 1964 had brought some peace but both sides had accused each other of violating it. The Underground charged the armed forces with continuing to target Naga villages and torturing their inhabitants. The Indian government accused the Underground of travelling to China to seek arms during the ceasefire period. The bomb blast destroyed the illusion of peace and progress in the new state of Nagaland. The road back to normalcy was long and painful. Every school held a condolence service for the students who had been killed in the blast. The ruins of the Ruby hall were cleared after many days and no attempt was made to build anything in its place for a long time.

The bomb blast saw an increase in the numbers of the armed police, the Central Reserve Police who nightly patrolled the town. They were a brutal lot who would beat up drunks and loiterers. Sometimes their methods emptied the streets of late-night carousers and sometimes the opposite could result. There were nights when young men defiantly drove their jeeps at great speed through town, tyres screeching and horns blaring in an open challenge to the armed police. In the months after the blast, women prayed that such a thing would never visit the town again.

Before the year ended, Vilhoulie suddenly died. He had been sick for some days. It was cirrhosis of the liver from all the years of alcohol abuse. He had been given many warnings by doctors before this last illness but he had never taken their advice to reduce his drinking. I was ashamed that I did not feel sad at the news of his death. At first, I felt relieved, and then shocked at my reaction. *Now he will no longer frighten us or other children*, that had been my first thought. I chided myself and tried to think of people who would be sad at his going. Maybe the friends who used to help him home. Maybe the women who sold him rice brew every evening in the drinking houses. But truly I could not bring myself to picture a scenario where his acquaintances and friends would be sad that he was gone.

As was our custom, the women in our neighbourhood made wreaths of pine branches and roses and gathered at his house. They all wore the black *lohe* cloth. Some women had hymnbooks with them and they sat down around the body in the parlour. Then they took out their hymnbooks and sang the sad, slow songs used only at funerals. I was surprised that an elderly woman was weeping loudly. She was the only one mourning him. Someone said she was his sister, a woman who had repeatedly tried to get him to stop drinking.

The pastor could not come but he sent the deacon to supervise the funeral. It was a brief funeral with the deacon reading out the dates of Vilhoulie's baptism and marriage in church, and the name of his late wife. He read some Bible verses and then announced that those gathered would now lay his mortal remains in the earth. Everyone present stood up as four of the men carried out the coffin to the grave that had been dug behind his house. The deacon said a prayer and they lowered the coffin inside the hole and covered it with soil. The deacon led the people in a hymn and then it was all over. Two men were waiting to put a wooden cross over the mound and as soon as people began to disperse, they stuck the cross with his name, dates of birth and death into the red soil. Then they hammered the cross a few times to be quite sure it would stay up.

I went home with a sense of awe. Vilhoulie had been such a fearful figure when he was alive and I had never thought my life would one day be free of him. Even when I turned the corner and went past his house I half expected him to jump out with a loud shout. I had to shake off the feeling and remind myself that he was lying under the earth and we would never see him again in this life. It would be like Atsa Bonuo and Ami Amo and Apuo who we never saw again when they died and were buried.

After his death, people claimed to have seen Vilhoulie or heard him shouting up the road. But I never once saw or heard him again.

FIFTEEN

Prohibition Talk and Others

In the months that followed, Vilhoulie's death opened up the debate on the drinking houses and if they should be allowed to operate. People had somehow come to accept that the drinking houses would always be a part of the town. The population had increased in leaps and bounds since the rebuilding of Kohima began in the forties. Some families lived on the income they made selling home-brewed local wine. Their children went to school and their mothers paid their fees with the money they earned selling brew. There were a few licensed liquor shops in the town as well. Still, drinking was frowned upon by the church and people like Vilhoulie, who had harassed law-abiding citizens, were often cited as examples for supporting the idea of prohibition. Certainly, the North Police station had a lock-up where alcoholics were confined for the night if they were making a nuisance of themselves. But the debate drew on the stories of those families where the men were using up their salaries on alcohol and had nothing left to support their families. This was the real problem for the affected families.

Some of the church members had heard about prohibition laws in America and wondered if it was possible to do the same in Nagaland.

'It's all very well for the Americans. But we can't do that here. The government is earning a revenue on the sale of liquor and may not be willing to cooperate. If anything is to change, it would have to come by way of a people's movement.' That was Lhouvitso, who was an educated man, so he understood how things worked in the government sector. 'Anyway, a person like Vilhoulie—everyone knew it was just a matter of time until he died an alcoholic death. I have heard that even in the drinking houses they didn't like to serve him because he would threaten to beat up customers when he had a drink or two inside him. Even the government cannot do anything to stop such people from drinking. And the church should be aware that it could land in legal problems if it tries to fight for prohibition. The point when drinking becomes a problem is when a man takes the money meant for his family and uses it on drink. That is when everyone has to say, stop! I should know. I used to do that.' That was how the debates ended with no group willing to take action, knowing the government would have the law on its side.

By and by, stories began to surface of wife-beatings. Azuo and Azuo Zeü were discussing the case of a young neighbour whose husband had returned from a drinking house and beaten her so badly that her family had taken her away.

'He had been hanging out with a group of young men and they were very violent. But the wife-beating had been going on for some time before.'

'I hear he's broken four of her ribs. Her face was so swollen I could not recognise her,' Azuo added. 'I hope she's not going back to him again after all that.'

'I think the family should do their best to prevent that happening. It is not a good system we have of sending girls back to husbands who are abusive. It's as good as sending them back to their deaths.' I was surprised to hear Azuo Zeü speak like that. I had always known her to be very conservative and keen to uphold what I considered as very rigid views.

'What should she do then?' Azuo asked with real concern. 'Once she is married, we consider her to be her husband's property.'

'And that is so wrong—that kind of thinking. The husband thinks he can do anything he wants with his wife, that he has the right to mistreat her and no one should say anything against it.' I had never heard Azuo Zeü sounding so agitated before. It took some minutes before she noticed I was in the room.

'Kevinuo, I would have asked you to go to your room because you are still so young. But maybe it's a good thing for you to start learning that there are hard things in life. This is what I want you to know—a man may say that he loves his wife dearly when he marries her, but the same man can become twisted by alcohol and even beat her. That has happened with our neighbours. Kevinuo, if you should ever marry such a man, remember that you are not his property for him to beat you and break your bones. This is probably not the kind of thing they would teach you in school. But you must learn this lesson from today. A man's responsibility is first and foremost, to provide food and shelter for his family. Then he should teach his children to be good citizens and try to be an example himself. In turn, his family members should respect and honour him. This is the way it is supposed to be. If people start beating each other, don't ever accept that as normal.'

I was very surprised by Azuo Zeü's words, but I listened attentively to every word and said yes. I had never given much thought to marriage. My world revolved around my studies and my future dream of going to college and someday getting a job. Marriage sounded frightening at my age. I was not interested in marrying although some of our classmates talked and talked about it. I certainly was not going to marry someone like our neighbour's husband who would beat me! Suddenly I remembered what Azuo Zeü had been telling me.

'She's not dead, is she?' I asked.

'Who? The woman? No, but if she goes back to him, she might as well be dead. No one in their right mind returns to a man who beats them.'

I crept to my room, a bit frightened of Azuo Zeü, but also grateful for all that she had taught me. As the older one in the family, I was used to being subjected to long lectures on how to behave culturally, how to address elders, and be considerate of others around us. But this was my first lecture on marriage and it sounded like a dreadful thing to me if your husband could walk into the house and start beating you. But then I remembered my parents and how happy they had been together in their brief marriage. I had never seen

Apuo beating Azuo or scolding her. Then that meant one thing—there did exist marriages where the partners were happy and good to each other.

I discussed it with Beinuo as soon as we met. She knew about the story of the neighbour couple as did many others. That sort of thing was not possible to keep hidden from one's neighbours.

'Azuo Zeü said that we should not have to put up with our husbands beating us when we are married,' I said.

'And she is quite right. Why should we be beaten when we sacrifice so much in a marriage?'

'We do?' I asked stupidly.

'Of course, we do. We leave our parents, our siblings, and our childhood homes behind. We have to start a new family and bear children and look after them. It's almost as though we enter into a life of slavery for the honour of being someone's wife.'

'You make it sound really awful,' I protested.

'Sorry, it's not all like that. It can be nice too, of course. The wife and husband may love each other very much and be willing to give up their families and be with each other all the time. Our neighbour's case is very different. Anyone can see he couldn't have loved her much if he could beat her so badly.'

'They said he had been hanging out with some rough friends lately and drinking in their company.'

'Why do people say things like that? That he was with this person or that person? They are putting the blame on someone else when they bring that up. I think the husband has to take responsibility for beating his wife instead of hiding behind his friends and his alcohol habit.' We both felt frustrated and affected by the sad story. The world of grown-ups was complicated and we felt ill-equipped for it. Beinuo seemed to be better informed on the matter than I. Of the two of us, she was ever the practical one.

'What would you do if your husband beat you?' I asked.

'I would beat him right back!' Beinuo answered without any hesitation. 'He has no right to beat me. I won't let him.'

SIXTEEN

Matriculation and College

In the year that Beinuo and I sat our matriculation examinations, Ato was studying in the sixth grade. Both Azuo and I monitored his lessons which had suddenly become much harder. He started to take tuition from the Mathematics teacher. Four times a week, the three of them—Ato, Chuba, and Nobin—went to the teacher's house after school hours. He was a strict but dedicated teacher and would not give up until they had thoroughly understood their lessons.

'It's all about concentration,' he had told my mother. 'These boys are at the age when it's almost impossible to get them to focus on a single thing. They are not stupid, just lazy and not used to working independently. Don't worry, they will show some improvement by next month.' True to his word, Ato's marks began to pick up. He was eleven years old and growing very fast. He was almost as tall as me. These days he spent more time with his friends playing football after school. Ato did not enjoy studying. But like the rest of us, he understood it was unavoidable if he wanted to have a good life.

'No girl will marry you if you don't pass High School,' Azuo liked to warn him.

'I don't want to marry. I just want to play as much football as I can. If there was a football playing school, I would go there.'

'Actually, there are schools where they teach you to become a good football player,' I said.

'Really? Can I go there?'

'If you want, but they are all in America, none here in Kohima.' He was disappointed but not for long. Ato was never worried about anything for long. Azuo reached out and pulled him to her.

'If you keep growing at this rate, I will have to lengthen your trousers or make you wear your father's old clothes,' Azuo remarked as she examined him. They had been to the tailor to make him a second pair of school pants before the year was out.

'Who's the tallest among you three?' Azuo asked.

'Chuba,' he answered. 'Nobin and I are about the same height, and I can reach Chuba's ear.'

'You will soon be as tall as him, don't worry,' Azuo said.

'One day I will be taller than you, Azuo,' Ato stated with a smile that ended as a smirk.

'Yes, you will. And you can take care of me when that day comes,' she replied.

As Ato and I grew older, Azuo no longer seemed to be as strong as she appeared to be in our childhood. She had remained thin all her life. In the pictures of her as a young girl, she looked slim and stylish. Nowadays her clothes hung on her and she looked older because of her grey hair. But she would still do the housework and the cooking on her own. Azuo was hoping to retire from work in another five years. Once a week, a woman came from the village to weed the garden and to help her with some of the household tasks. I helped in the morning with sweeping the rooms and swabbing the floors. After that it was a rush to get to school.

When the matriculation results were declared in June, Beinuo and I found our names in the roll of those who had passed. We were so happy, we ran home from school and told our parents. The headmistress summoned all of us the next day to congratulate us and give out the numbers of those who had passed. She wished us very well in our future life and hoped that we would all continue studying. She said that ours had been a very good batch, that we had scored higher marks than our seniors and we should not give up studies if our parents were able to support us. With her words of praise ringing in our ears we went home, very pleased with ourselves.

'Maybe she says that to every batch that passes out from school,' one of our friends remarked.

'We don't care, do we?' another friend retorted. 'We must be good if the headmistress herself says so. I'm going to get admitted to college as soon as my mark sheets arrive.'

'Can't we get admitted already?'

'Oh, yes. I think they can give something called provisional admissions before our mark sheets arrive.'

'Really? If that is possible, we don't have to waste time waiting.' We enthusiastically made plans to meet the next day and visit Kohima College and find out. I rushed home and told Azuo what my friends had said.

'I know what she is talking about. It is called provisional admission based on the expectation that your results will be successful. We can go to the college tomorrow.' It was very exciting and I was grateful Azuo was ready to take me to the college and find out. I ran to Beinuo's house and told her. We decided to go together in the morning. Her father would be busy the next day, but we agreed that if my mother came with us, she could speak to the Principal for both of us. We were neither of us worried because we had both passed.

The next morning Azuo took us to the college. We were not the only ones. Many of our classmates were there as well, especially the ones who were intending to continue studying in Kohima.

'Kevinuo! Beinuo!' Our friends from school were calling out our names from the far corner of the wooden building that housed Kohima College. We waved at them and followed Azuo into the Principal's office. He was a jovial looking man from the Ao tribe.

'Come in, come in and tell me your names,' he boomed in a loud voice. 'You say they have both passed?' he asked my mother. She replied that the school had our roll numbers and names in the first list.

'Well, it's no problem. You can get admitted today and tomorrow you can join classes for the pre-university first year.' Beinuo and I stole glances at each other. We couldn't believe we were about to become college students. Not only was the Kohima College the first college offering Arts subjects, it was also the only college in town. Azuo thanked him and so did we and he ushered us out of his office so we could pay our admission fees at the office counter.

Outside his office, there was a long line of parents waiting to meet him. They had all come to get their children and wards admitted. The window of one of the classrooms was open. I put my head in to look and stepped back immediately. A man with a beard was holding forth about the First World War. He grinned when he saw how embarrassed I was to be caught poking my head into his classroom.

The next day we showed up at the college early. The bearded teacher came into our class, and he introduced himself as the lecturer for History. He was friendly and asked us our names and wanted to know what we intended to do with our college degree. The question was rather unexpected and we blushed and stammered when asked to give our answers.

'Do you know these very buildings housed the hospital before the war?' the History teacher asked when he first entered our class. Not everyone was aware of that. 'Well, that was thirty years ago. The houses were much better then, and they even conducted minor surgery in these rooms.' We were all very surprised at that.

'There were both white doctors and Naga doctors. And the houses were in a much better condition then,' he laughed as he said this. The wooden floors in some of the classrooms were now badly in need of repair.

'The hospital was shifted to its present site after the war and the buildings were given to the Government Middle English School. When the school vacated the premises, the college moved into the empty rooms. That's a little on the history of your college for you to remember although you won't be asked to write about it in your examinations,' he added with a broad smile.

Classes started every day at 9.30; unlike school, there was no assembly before classes. Some students showed up late and ambled into the classroom without giving any excuses for their lateness. The apparent lack of discipline dismayed us. College life looked like it was going to be very different from school life.

Our class was the biggest with about 200 new students. Latecomers never found a seat and some of the boys took to sitting on the windowsill or on the floor. Getting to class early in order to ensure you got a seat was a good incentive to be punctual. After a few weeks, our class was divided into two sections; the majority of the girls remained in the first section and didn't have to move to the other classroom.

As the days went by, we learned that students lacking a high enough percentage of attendance would not be allowed to appear their examinations. Towards the end of the year, many new faces joined our class. As it turned out, they had all been admitted around the same time as us, and the approaching examination was behind their eagerness to make up for the loss in attendance.

The college was in the heart of the town and several tea stalls had sprouted nearby because the students bought tea and snacks during breaks.

It was an exciting phase of our lives. After weeks of attending classes, we were told to fill up scholarship forms in order to receive money which the government distributed to students who came from low income families. Both Beinuo and I were eligible for the scholarship and we proudly took home four hundred rupees each when the money came.

'*Hou!* To pay you to study is too generous of the government!' Azuo exclaimed when I brought home the money. 'You keep that for yourself and buy some clothes and shoes,' she said and refused to take it. I felt that I was beginning to support myself and it was great to feel so independent. Beinuo said she had bought four bags of charcoal as her contribution to the family expenses. I wanted to do the same thing so I paid the milk bill in the coming months. We were told we would get scholarships at regular intervals and we could instruct the office to deduct our fees before the payment. I told Azuo about it and she said it would be as though I was putting myself through college. We all thought it was a wonderful opportunity.

College life had other things in store for us besides the academic workload that we were daily given. After the rains cleared in autumn, the college sports week was arranged by the Students' Union and it was compulsory for every student. At the end of the activities the teachers would take attendance. The sports week was conducted with the aim of inspiring athletes for the inter-college sports that would follow. We were surprised to see the level of professionalism with which the sports week was held. In the inter-college sports competition, our college football team scored over the Science college team from Jotsoma. Soon the news came that they had qualified to participate in the North Eastern Hill University sports week at Shillong. It was a wonder that we could have an academic life in the midst of all these exciting interruptions. Our team came back from Shillong with the sad news that they could not get to the finals, but it was still a matter of pride that they had qualified for the University sports week.

In November, almost without any preparation, we sat for our first set of pre-university examinations. It was a qualifying exam for the main university examinations in April and May. Beinuo and I spent our long winter break with our church group at choir practice and decorating the church for Christmas. Azuo Zeü asked when I was going to start studying, and I guiltily admitted that I was waiting for Christmas to be over. Friends of ours said that it was quite normal to be done with the celebrations before settling down to serious cramming for the exams. There was a lot to study and the subjects, except for History and English, were nothing connected to what we had studied in school. Our classmates worried that our papers would go to external examiners in Shillong who would be very strict with marking. The pressure of exams came from a combination of trying to study as much as possible in a short period and the anxiety over not meeting the expectations of our examiners.

The years at college passed in this manner: there was an abiding sense that we were short of time for everything that was happening in our lives. Winter breaks were not long enough; study preparations could have gone better with an extra week and made all the difference to our performances. I always regretted not studying more, not starting a few days earlier than I actually had. It showed in my average grades when my mark sheets came. But there was no opportunity to improve my marks as I had already passed the final exams. Other things in my life needed my attention.

SEVENTEEN

Ato and Other Rumblings

When I started at college, Ato was in the seventh standard. His four years at High School were turbulent, to put it mildly. As he hit adolescence he worried about his skin and clothes. He had an outbreak of acne that made a big dent in his confidence.

'It's only a phase,' I tried to comfort him. 'Look at me, I had acne in my second year and wanted to hide my face every time I went to class. But now it has cleared and I don't worry about my skin anymore.' But he would stand in front of the mirror for hours fretting. The two of us spent less time together because he was playing football regularly after classes. I had also been absorbed in my own world at college. His football playing meant that he would come home late and go to bed early, exhausted from the game. They increased the practice sessions from three evenings a week to four evenings. Mother worried that it would interfere with his studies.

'You're a High School student. You have to study much

harder than before,' she would nag. Poor Ato. He was finding out that growing up was not so easy. He was not used to working hard and struggled with trying to catch up with his studies so that he wouldn't have to sacrifice his football evenings. Both Nobin and Chuba were star footballers so we could well understand that he wanted to become a good player. It was a game in itself, trying to balance the two most important aspects of his life when each one demanded so much of his time and energy.

Azuo was exasperated every time he brought home his report card. Very low marks in Mathematics and most of the other subjects. In fact, the only subjects in which he had scored high marks were English and Scripture. It would have been funny if it wasn't so worrying, especially for Azuo.

'Maybe you can become a teacher of English? Or a Scripture teacher? You certainly won't be hired to teach any other subject if they see these marks!' She said this to remind him that when he was eight or nine he had always maintained he was going to be a teacher. It had been a cute thing coming from a small boy and Azuo liked to tell our visitors about it. 'Maybe he can become a PT teacher,' I remarked. It sounded ludicrous because no school had such a position. The sports department had a few openings for coaches, but at school our Physical Training teacher was one of the regular teachers who took other classes as well. We hadn't heard of schools hiring teachers to teach only PT.

'I don't have to be a teacher. I can set up a shop like Nobin's father,' Ato responded.

'Nobin's father is a successful businessman. He has a very popular music shop besides the other shops he owns. You're

not a music-lover. What would you sell, my son? Footballs?'
Azuo laughed. The picture of himself sitting in a shop
adjacent to Nobin's father's shop and selling footballs caused
Ato to break out into a big smile.

'Listen, Ato,' Azuo broke in, 'one day Kevinuo will marry
and go away from us because she is a girl. She will live in her
husband's house and start her own family. But you will always
be here even if you get married.' Your wife will make this
house her home and you will have children. That's why you
need to have a job, earn money and provide for your wife and
children. That's how life is. You are studying so that you can
get a job.' Ato looked dismayed for some moments.

'I'm not sure I can do all that. I just want to play football
every day of my life.'

'That is what you want now, but a time will come when
you will wish you had played less football and studied more.
I am telling you now so you won't make the wrong choices
later.' That was how Azuo's talks with Ato went. She became
a teacher all over again. But it had some effect on him and
he managed to pass his exams even if he had below average
marks. When I was studying for my Bachelor exams, he was
preparing for his matriculation examinations.

'When you pass your matric exams, you can start at
college,' I said.

'And do what? Study more?' he didn't look at all excited
at that prospect. It came as no big surprise to the rest of our
family that Ato did not want to go to college. Since we could
not possibly force him to study further, we had to do the
next best thing and that was to discuss his options. It turned
out that he really did want to run a shop though he was not

clear what he wanted to sell. He liked the idea of owning a sports shop in town and he was also attracted to opening a restaurant serving Chinese food.

'Ato, you are still very young. How old are you? Sixteen?' Azuo Zeü asked.

'Yes, and I will be 17 in the middle of the year,' he said.

'Why not get some training while you are waiting? If you still want to start a shop at the end of your training, we will support you and help you to start a shop. As it happens, I know the owners of the stationery store near the NST station. They have been wanting to close the stationery store and rent out the premises. I can talk to them. But first, you should enrol in a vocational course of your choice.'

Ato agreed to Azuo Zeü's plan and was admitted to the Industrial Training Institute on the High School road. When it was first established it was called the Junior Polytechnic School. The institute offered courses in Carpentry, Blacksmithy, Motor Mechanics, and Electronics for its male students. Ato began attending Carpentry and Motor Mechanics courses and surprised us all when his training was underway. I think he surprised himself as well because he enjoyed working with his hands so much that he would be reluctant to stop in the middle of a project when it was closing time. The months passed swiftly for him and he was eager to learn more. He came home late trailing wood shavings all over Azuo's clean floors. But she learned not to complain as she had realised that he was finally doing something that he truly liked and she was grateful for it.

I sometimes think of the look my dying father had given me when we stood at his bedside; it was a silent plea to look after my brother and I had tried to fulfil that duty. Ato finding his place in life made me feel greatly relieved and, in a way, I know that the sense of relief was connected to not failing my father.

When Ato was in the third year of his training, Beinuo confided in me that she had received a marriage proposal. It was not a surprise as we were both at the age considered marriageable by our aunts and female relatives. He was a boy who had been after her from our first year at college, but Beinuo had not been interested then. Now she seemed to find the idea attractive enough to consider accepting his offer. I was a little heartbroken because she was my closest friend. We had been together throughout school and college and shared so much. Nonetheless, I knew this was inevitable, that one day one of us or both of us would marry and start our separate lives.

Beinuo had a small wedding in November. It was a private affair where only the two families and a few friends were invited. I didn't get to be her bridesmaid as the wedding did not take place in church; the pastor came to their house and conducted the wedding in the parlour.

'We're still best friends, you know,' she comforted me. 'You must come over as often as you can. Promise me that you will come?' she pleaded.

'Of course I will, silly,' I responded. 'It's not likely that I will go out and find another friend to replace you. Where would I find anyone as wise and as smart and as daft as you?' We were both crying.

'Oh, why did you have to get married?' I blurted out because I was still a bit angry with her.

'You hurry up and get married as well and then you will find out why I got married,' she smiled. I had little idea how long she had been seeing her husband before they decided to marry. She would have told me because we were still doing things together after college even though she had taken up a job as a Lower Divisional Clerk in the Deputy Commissioner's office and I had my teaching job, but we made it a point to catch up at weekends and do stuff together. She did say he used to send her messages through mutual friends asking to go out with her. But she did not encourage him because she wanted to do well at her job and earn lots of money so she didn't have to live at home. Beinuo told me he was very persistent and she gradually came round to the idea that it would not be a bad thing at all to get married and have her own house. Her plan of saving money to build her own house would take years. In addition, she had become fond of her suitor so they went ahead and married.

I didn't know what to make of her husband, Meselhou. He was a little reserved and kept to himself but the fact that he had been so determined for years to make Beinuo his wife won our admiration. He owned an automobile repair shop and his widowed mother would often be seen sitting in the shop selling motor parts. It was their family business. Beinuo and Meselhou moved into an annexe in their compound. Meselhou was the only son in the family and he would inherit the ancestral house, but he had two unmarried sisters who were still waiting for their turn to be married. Moving into the annexe was to give the newlyweds some privacy and allow Beinuo to run her household the way she wanted.

I visited them a few weeks after the wedding. The annexe had a small and cosy sitting room, two bedrooms and a kitchen where she had already arranged her utensils and crockery. I asked her how married life was and she said she was learning much about coping with a new family and fitting in. 'But are you happy?' I insisted. 'I'm sure I am,' she replied. It was such an odd reply. I thought about it afterwards and wondered if I wanted to get married at all if it entailed so many adjustments with new people. In the months that followed, I would hear Beinuo say, 'That's not the way my mother-in-law does it' or 'Meselhou doesn't like it that way.' She seemed anxious to please her in-laws and that was only natural to an extent. But it made me sad that the vibrant girl I had known seemed to have disappeared altogether and another person had taken her place.

With Beinuo married, I was pressured by my father's relatives to get married too.

'Don't put it off too long. You modern girls want to wait and wait but if you wait too long, you'll find out no one wants an old maid.'

There is a time for everything. In a person's life, there is a time to marry. It is good to marry when the time is right for it. I grew used to hearing things like these especially at family gatherings or friends' weddings. I usually laughed them off, but ours was such a small society that when a girl got a proposal from a man, everyone got to hear about it. When the girl rejected the man, that too became public information. Marriage was a community affair. Most of them knew I had turned down two of the men who proposed to me. My grand aunt Nisoü thought I had made a big mistake with the second man who worked at the Public Works Department. They couldn't understand that I needed to know the person better if I were to commit to marriage; it was not enough to simply find out his earning prospects.

In the meantime, Beinuo got pregnant and we spent some Saturdays together knitting baby clothes.

'Do you think it will be a boy?' she asked.

'I have no idea whether it'll a boy or a girl. A healthy and normal child will be wonderful, don't you think?' I replied.

'I hope it's a boy. Meselhou's family needs boys to take on the family business after him.'

'And if it's a girl, will they be angry?'

'Of course not,' she said. 'They are quite pleased about my pregnancy.'

Beinuo had a normal pregnancy and was able to carry her baby to full term. When her pains started, she was admitted to the Naga Hospital and in the evening, she delivered a baby girl. I wanted to see her the next morning but couldn't get leave as we were conducting examinations for the senior classes. I had to wait until evening. She was there with her baby but no sign of the baby's father.

'Where's Meselhou?' I asked.

'I'm not sure. He hasn't been in the whole day.' Beinuo looked sad and confused.

'Is he sick? He must be sick if he hasn't been in today,' I reasoned.

'No, he is not sick,' she said in a very low tone. I almost did not hear her.

'What's wrong, Beinuo? Have you two quarrelled?' I had to ask.

'No,' she said and looked away. I saw her shoulders heaving and knew she was crying.

'Oh no, what is wrong? Please tell me what's wrong?'

'He is not happy that the baby is a girl.' I was exasperated when I heard her answer. I looked down at the sweet little thing in the crib. Everything about her was perfect. When she reached out her hand I caught it in mine and her fingers twirled around my thumb trustingly. How could anyone be angry at this?

'I can't believe what you are saying. I hope it's just a joke. Look at her! How can anyone be angry she is not a boy? Look, Beinuo, just look at your daughter! She is perfect and you have nothing to be ashamed of. If Meselhou is going to be a fool, I'll tell him a thing or two.'

'No no, you mustn't do that. Please, Kevinuo, promise me you won't. I will sort this out. We will sort it out. It's our problem. I'm a married woman now.' She stressed the last phrase and gave me a look. I think that look was the reason why I backed off and kept my distance in the months that followed. The look said, *please don't interfere,* and I felt she was closing off a door that I used to enter easily in the past without ever bothering to knock.

The baby girl was named Melouvinuo after her grand aunt. She was a petite little thing and had been very sick in the weeks after her birth and they feared for her survival. She was admitted to hospital with fever and a cough which the hospital diagnosed as Croup. The little one struggled to breathe through her blocked airways, and her mother cried as she watched her child suffering. After four days she pulled through and they were discharged from the hospital. In the following weeks her appetite returned and she doubled her size, which wasn't really all that much. But she was much healthier now and her mother tried to be less anxious over her. Everyone close to her began calling her Uvi as her full name, Melouvinuo, was quite a mouthful.

EIGHTEEN

Azuo

At the end of his training period, Ato was 20 years old and already doing some side business as a carpenter. He had well developed muscles from the hard work of his daily training and he had grown much taller. The little brother that I used to look out for now no longer needed me to be his guardian angel. I felt old. I was 25 and had been teaching at the government school for three years. Seeing Ato work at his training, I felt I needn't worry anymore about what he would do with his life.

With Beinuo I couldn't help worrying but, in a way, I felt she had pushed me out of her life and though I visited her once a month, I had long since stopped enquiring about her relationship with her husband. She was very changed from the old Beinuo that I used to know. There was something about her that I couldn't quite put my finger on. One day I was shopping at the April Showers store when she walked in with her sister-in-law. I called out and approached them excitedly, but she seemed to be in a hurry to get her shopping done. She answered my queries after Uvi so distractedly that I began to feel I was in the way. I moved back and bid them goodbye and she looked relieved when I did that.

It hurt me very much that my closest friend had chosen to distance herself from me like this. We had been closer than sisters, never having kept any secrets from each other, and now we exchanged greetings like acquaintances, not friends. Beinuo had become so evasive that I found myself sometimes dreading the monthly visit to her house. *I'm doing it for Uvi*, I would try to convince myself. At least the little girl was very fond of me and ran to me every time I visited. I loved her dearly and enjoyed finding out the new words she had learned.

'Hello, what's your name?' I asked the first time she was learning to speak. She giggled and shook her head and then said quite clearly, 'Uvi.' I made her repeat it over and over again. 'Uvi, Uvi, Uvi' she called out and ran off to her mother and ran back to me.

One day, when I was alone with Beinuo, I asked, 'Listen, do you want me to stop coming?' The question caught her by surprise and she exclaimed, 'Of course not, what made you think that?'

I didn't answer. She asked me the same question again.

'It's because every time I come here, I feel I am unwanted, I feel like I am in the way here in your house.'

'Don't ever think that please. I have no one if you don't come by.' After saying that she looked very unhappy. 'Don't let anyone know I said that,' she whispered. I couldn't understand her situation. Why didn't her family visit her? Her stepsisters could come by but they never did. Maybe if we met outside the house she might tell me more, I thought.

'We could go for a shopping tour one of these days. I need to buy some winter clothing. You could bring Uvi and help me pick up some nice sweaters,' I suggested.

'Meselhou doesn't like me to take Uvi to the shops. They're too crowded and she could get an infection.' There it was again, the evasiveness. Each time I stretched forth a hand, she drew back, and whenever I tried to go away from her, she pulled me back in her mild way, like that little admission that she had no one if I were to stop coming by. I suspected that things were not quite right between the two of them and wondered why they did not work on it. It was not like Beinuo to be so passive. At least not the Beinuo that I used to know.

'You could come on your own. Your mother-in-law can look after Uvi for an hour or two. It won't take long,' I coaxed her.

'I'm sorry, Mother does not like it if I leave Uvi and go out on my own.' I didn't ask her again. I didn't have time to.

My own life became quite chaotic when Azuo had a fall from the steps leading to Azuo Zeü's house and broke her ankle in two places. She was hospitalised and Ato and I had to stop everything else and do hospital duty in turns. Azuo hated that she was the cause of disrupting the routine of our lives. She didn't stay in hospital more than a week and came home with a plaster cast. Using one crutch, she hobbled around the house, insisting that she was much improved. Ato returned to his training but I took more leave from school.

'You don't have to extend your leave,' she protested. 'I can look after myself. You see how well I get around the house with my crutch.'

'I know, Azuo, and I do see it. The leave is for me, not for you. I will take a long well-deserved rest using you as an excuse,' I said. She quietened down after that and tried to look after me instead! That was so typical of her. In the afternoons when everything was calmer, I made tea for us and we sat and had long chats, something we had not done for a long time.

'For my sake, I would like to see you married and settled before I die.' Azuo had started on this theme a couple of years ago when Apuo's relatives nagged her to do something about her unmarried daughter. They felt that I was getting too close to the age when spinsterhood would become inevitable.

'You are only 51, Azuo, not 80. You won't die now and I am not sure I want to get married yet,' I replied.

'Did you hear me say 'for my sake'? I would want you to be happy with someone as your father and I were happy. But that is something I wish for my own sake. You may be quite happy being on your own. I do consider that too.'

It was hard to take a decision on marriage. I did not want to be alone all my life. At the same time, to become trapped like Beinuo in a marriage with a controlling partner was not what I wanted at all.

'What if we find a wife for Ato instead?' I asked jokingly. 'He is getting old enough to marry. Apuo and you were not so much older than him when you got married,' I teased her.

'What do you mean? Not much older than Ato? Oh no, we were much older and we knew without a shadow of doubt that we wanted to spend our lives together. Hmm, come to think of it, I was nearly 25 when we married. I was almost a spinster by then! All the friends I grew up with were married and they teased me at every opportunity. But I waited because I believed that someone as fine as your father would show up. And until he did, it would be such a mistake to be pushed into marriage with somebody who was wrong for me. Kevinuo, perhaps you should just wait. Let that dream man of yours come along and you'll find the wait was worth it all.'

My marital status had become a private joke between us. Boys I knew at school were all married now and even had children. When we bumped into each other, they would encourage their kids to call me *Ania*, paternal aunt.

'Only a rich, old widower would come asking for my hand now,' I joked.

'Well, we never know. He might be worth waiting for,' she replied.

Azuo's ankle took months to heal completely. She naturally grew very cautious about putting her weight on it even though the doctor said it would be okay. She was still as thin as ever but that proved to be a blessing in disguise as she did not have to worry about overstraining her ankle. The doctor said if she had been heavier she would have taken a longer time to recover. She used the crutch every time she left the house. She joked about how dependent she had become on the crutch and waved it about shouting, 'This is my new husband!'

I had gone back to work after the extra week of leave. Azuo Zeü kept her promise of keeping Azuo company when we were not in the house. I would come home to the smell of good food and the sound of laughter as the two sisters made warm meals for us to share. Fish soup was supposed to be very good for any injury. We fed Azuo plenty of fish soup and country ginger. She avoided garlic, chicken, and beef; pork was recommended by our people and many times family members brought local pork for her. I'm sure all these varieties of food also worked towards her healing as did time and patience. It was almost Christmastime when Azuo decided to stop using her crutch.

'You can use a cane in the beginning,' I suggested but she was totally against that.

'Anyone can see that a person using a crutch has had an injury, but a cane would age me and I do not want people running to me to help a little old lady,' she stated firmly. Her first walks without her crutch were awkward. She still tended to reach out for support even though she could walk quite well. A few training walks back and forth to Azuo Zeü's house and down the lane improved her confidence. On Christmas day, she walked straight-backed up the church courtyard waving away the hands that were stretched out to help her climb up the steps.

I was the tense one, walking beside her and readying to catch her if she should stumble. But Azuo confidently walked into our usual pew and sat down, smiling and nodding to people she knew. I saw that Beinuo and her family were seated a few pews ahead of us, but beyond a smile and a wave, we couldn't really talk. During my mother's convalescence she had sent some money though she had never come to the house herself. I should go over and thank her for that, I told myself.

After the service was done, I approached her and thanked her for her gift. Meselhou was standing beside her. I held out my hand in greeting and when he leaned over to shake my hand, I smelt the unmistakable whiff of rice brew. I was surprised as it was rather early in the day to start drinking. Beinuo looked awkward when I mentioned the money. 'Please, it was such a small amount. I should have come to help but I didn't have anyone to look after the baby,' she said. Only then did I see she had had another child. I congratulated them and gave my apologies for not visiting. She smiled and told me not to worry. Beinuo was wearing a new coat. Her hair was parted to the side and it suited her. But she looked drawn and painfully thin.

'Are you staying for the feast?' I asked them. They pointed to the baby in her arms and excused themselves. There was no invitation to their house for me from either of them.

NINETEEN

Beinuo

In the new year, Ato opened a new shop. It was really an extension of the old shop and he set it up because the business had grown and he needed more space. At 21, Ato was one of the youngest entrepreneurs in town. He had a clientele that patronised him on account of his extreme youth and his knowledge of mechanical things. He had stayed with his dream of owning a sports shop. In the extended area he sold carpentry tools and automobile parts. Ato's customers were a mixture of young boys and girls, sports enthusiasts and car owners, and older men who liked to do a bit of carpentry themselves. The shop was rarely empty. Peak hours for Ato were the after-school hours. He quickly realised that he needed an assistant and he hired a Bengali who used to work in Dimapur in a similar shop. Between the two of them, they handled the rush hour quite adroitly and the shop's reputation spread by word of mouth.

Ato's former critics were now full of praise for him and for Azuo. They said that she was a clever woman and that Ato had taken the right step by not continuing in a line where he wouldn't have been happy. They wanted to introduce their sons to Ato so he could mentor them. Some of those boys were so frustrated with their lives that they were drinking heavily. Boys hardly out of their teens. Alcohol abuse was becoming a problem in the younger generation as well. The drinking houses selling rice-brew did not have any age restrictions and younger boys had access to these drinking houses. People also said that the general frustration with life was driving men to drink more in the present decade. They were quick to blame the political situation, the brutality of army occupation, the transition from rural to modern which left some people out in the cold because they did not have enough education or skills, the heavy migration from the rural areas to the townships, and the problems of sharing resources among an ever-increasing population. And they were right on all counts. The government lacked a support system for the affected families, whether it was in terms of financial or psychological support.

Some people put forward the view that this was a problem for the church to solve. But the roots of alcoholism were so complicated that the church felt handicapped by the complex nature of the problem. Still, it could not ignore the broken families and battered wives that were a direct fallout of alcoholism. Using the method of tough love, some churches began to excommunicate drinking members. It was a big mistake. It threw up the whole debate on salvation. If the church closed its doors, would heaven close its doors too? Wasn't salvation about grace for sinners? Didn't Jesus have mercy on the sinners of his day? What right did the church have to excommunicate a man because he drank? Wasn't it the duty of the church to be Christ-like and help people who were struggling with alcoholism? Every argument seemed to go in favour of the alcoholics.

The church maintained that alcohol abuse was behind many of the social problems in the state. The families of alcoholics were starving because the man of the house was using his salary to pay debts accrued in the drinking houses. The same men would go home and beat their wives if they berated them for not bringing home money. Convinced of the interconnection between the sale of alcohol and domestic abuse, the church moved the state to pass the Liquor Prohibition Act. It led to violent confrontations between the drinking house women and the women from the church when the church women went into the drinking houses and overturned the brew stored in big pots. The church women congratulated themselves on their show of zeal in destroying the works of the devil, but there were men who prophesied that prohibition would only push the sales of alcohol underground.

'They did the same thing in America and it didn't work. First the government enforced prohibition. Almost immediately the mafia became involved in smuggling alcohol across states and selling it at very high profit. Prohibition is a very bad idea. It has never worked before.' But no one listened to these men. The licensed liquor shops were the first to go. They shut down temporarily and reopened as automobile parts sales counters. The drinking houses were raided and closed down for some weeks.

But smuggling was easier than people realised. Even before the state legislature finally passed the Prohibition Act, smugglers had begun a very profitable trade of selling liquor to enthusiastic buyers. At strategic corners, shops masquerading as *paan* shops became selling points for smuggled alcohol. The price of beer and spirits doubled and tripled. The profits were so tempting that many small players entered the business of transporting alcohol from the neighbouring state of Assam to sell in Nagaland.

Did prohibition stop alcoholism? The answer was a resounding no. Alcoholics continued to drink, they continued to find ways of feeding their addiction, and they made the best customers for the smugglers. Prohibition had pushed up the price of smuggled alcohol; yet even that was not sufficient incentive for drinkers to stop.

After the Prohibition Act was imposed, a new development was the deaths of alcoholics. A number of men died in quick succession. We knew some of them and the others we had never heard of. We thought it was simply a coincidence that these men had all died around the same time. But one of Ato's customers enlightened him on the real situation.

'No one is connecting these deaths to the recent prohibition in the state. But the truth is that the smuggled alcohol these men have been drinking is greatly adulterated. A friend of mine, a food inspector, has analysed samples of smuggled alcohol and he discovered a very high content of methanol and other substances. Even kerosene in some cases. No wonder there have been so many deaths. It was the methanol poisoning them and not just the alcohol in their bloodstream that's killing them. But this problem can no longer be tackled by the state because it has officially become a dry state. It no longer has any official authority to investigate alcohol-related deaths.'

We were shocked by these revelations but we could not be blind to the fact that more and more men were dying, all of them heavy drinkers. In the days before prohibition, men like Vilhoulie had lived very long in spite of their addictive drinking habits. After prohibition, the majority of men dying from alcohol abuse were in their thirties and forties.

Word came out that Meselhou was drinking heavily. That sort of thing did not go unnoticed for long in our small community. I awkwardly planned a visit to Beinuo. The new baby was a good excuse and I could take them a gift, but I hesitated because they had been so formal the time we had seen each other at church. As I was hesitating, we got news one morning that the baby had suddenly died. I dressed and rushed over to Beinuo's house. It was a cold morning and the skies were overcast so the house looked quite bleak. People who had heard of the tragedy had already come to help them prepare the funeral. Young people were at work setting up chairs in their courtyard and the clink of spades against stone could be heard from the road. It was the sound of grave digging.

I hurried inside the house. The baby had been laid out in the parlour in a little crib. There were many flowers at the foot of the crib. Beinuo and her mother-in-law were sitting beside the crib weeping inconsolably. When she saw me, she held out her hands to me and without any hesitation I hugged her and held the cold little hands.

'I'm so sorry, Beinuo,' I began. 'This is such a shock. How did this happen?'

'Meningitis,' she said between sobs, 'He had fever and was not feeding properly. We took him to the hospital the next day because he would not stop throwing up. But he died within an hour. There was nothing the doctors could do.' She began to sob again and I held her and let her cry.

Meselhou was nowhere to be seen. People kept filing into the room to look at the baby and mourn him. 'Our child, our child,' one of Meselhou's aunts kept calling over and over, stroking the infant's cheek and weeping loudly. I continued to sit beside Beinuo making sure she was not exhausting herself.

A young girl came to me and said, 'Please bring her into the bedroom so she can eat something.' I tried to persuade her to come with me and eat, but she refused to leave the baby.

'I won't see him again in this life. I can eat later, please don't make me leave him.' I sent the girl away saying I would make sure she was okay. Funerals for young children were always held the same day. The deacon had already come and they were waiting for the family to compose themselves. But where was Uvi? I had not seen her since I came in the door. Just at that moment, Meselhou came in with Uvi trailing behind him. She had been crying. Her eyes were red-rimmed and the moment she saw me she ran to me. 'Azuo Kevi!' she cried and locked her little arms around my neck as she sobbed her heart out. What could I say? It will be all right? No. Uvi didn't deserve to be lied to. I just held her until her sobbing subsided. Then I wiped her eyes and nose and she stayed in my lap, quite spent. This was the first death she had ever seen.

'She loved her brother so much. She would not let him out of her sight and was very worried when we had to take him to hospital. And now he is gone. My poor little Uvi,' Beinuo started to cry again.

The deacon cleared his throat and stood up. 'We are now ready to start the funeral service. We will give the family some time to say goodbye to their beloved child before we start. I request all the mourners to step outside while the family says their goodbyes to the departed.' The mourners filed out of the room and I stood up to go when Beinuo pulled at my skirt and said, 'Stay.' Uvi was still holding onto my hand and I sat back and drew her close.

'Uvi, come and say goodbye to your brother,' Beinuo spoke in a clear voice.

'Where are they taking him?' Uvi asked fearfully.

'He'll go to live with the angels and Jesus in heaven,' her mother replied. Uvi hesitated just a bit and then came forward and kissed her brother's forehead. Then she buried her face in my shoulder and her little body was wracked with sobs. It was heart-breaking.

They buried the baby in the back garden and afterwards the small grave was covered with soil, and the flowers that people had brought were arranged over the grave. I wanted to stay over and help but it had become awkward again. Beinuo had withdrawn into herself and looked fearful every time Meselhou entered the room. I left after promising Uvi I would come back again very soon. I was not aware then that I would be keeping that promise much sooner than I wanted.

A week after the baby died, Ato came home earlier than usual.

'Kevinuo, Beinuo is in the hospital. You had better go. I have heard that it's quite serious.'

'What happened?' I asked.

'No time for that. Just get ready and go. She has asked

for you. Get ready please, she could go any time.' I put on
my clothes in a daze and grabbed a taxi to take me to the
hospital. Beinuo was barely conscious when I reached. Half
her face and her left eye was covered in gauze bandages. She
kept blinking her right eye.

'Beinuo, it's Kevinuo. Can you see me?' I asked.

'Kevi, you came.' Her face began to crumple when she
saw me. A nurse rushed in and gave me a hard stare.

'Don't upset her. We're doing everything we can to stabilise
her condition.' I assured the nurse I would be heedful and
added that she had asked for me.

'You're her sister?' the hard-faced nurse asked.

'We're not related. I am her best friend,' I hoped they
wouldn't throw me out if I rendered that information.

'Don't stay long and don't upset her.' I knelt down to be
able to hear her better.

'Kevinuo, can you ever forgive me? I couldn't bring myself
to tell you the truth,' Beinuo was saying.

'Hush, there is nothing to forgive. I love you. I want you to
concentrate on getting better so you can be a good mother to
Uvi. She needs you. We all need you.'

'I haven't got much time. I want to tell you all. I was
wrong all along but I was afraid to tell you because you would
get angry and you would insist that I leave him. He started
beating me soon after we were married. It was always over
something I had done wrong. I kept avoiding you because I
was always afraid you would find me some day with bruises
or a black eye. He blamed me for losing Uvi's brother and
gave me the beating of my life. Then he pushed me down the
steps. I know I won't survive this, but I want you to promise

you will take Uvi away from him. He has destroyed my life but you mustn't let him destroy Uvi's life. She doesn't deserve it.'

I was struggling to let it all sink in. It was unbelievable but why would Beinuo lie to me? Her bruises were partially visible through the gauze; the skin was so swollen it looked as though it might burst.

'Why didn't you leave, Beinuo? Why? You know women can leave abusive marriages.'

'I couldn't. I was so afraid that others would condemn me. I didn't want to be a failure as a wife; it would affect Uvi all her life. It was too late by the time the beatings started. I did try once but I was already pregnant with Uvi and he threatened to find us both and kill us if I ever left him. *I will kill your baby in front of you,* he said. I didn't doubt that he would. I have lived in fear all my married life. Can you ever forgive me?'

'Stop asking that, you silly old thing,' I said trying to sound light because I didn't want her to get upset again. 'I'll protect Uvi with my life, and you are going to get better and we are going to walk out of this hospital together.' She smiled weakly and tried to move her hand, but the movement made her wince. It alarmed me.

'What is it, Beinuo? Where does it hurt? Tell me so I can help you.'

'I moved too quickly. My rib…'

'Lie back in a comfortable position. Do you want me to call the nurse?'

'No.' I pulled a low stool towards the bed so I could continue sitting close to her.

'Do you want anything to eat?'

'No.'

Her right eye began to blink rapidly and that was when I noticed her nose was bleeding. She had bled into the white pillow cover. I shouted for the nurse while grabbing a gauze bandage to staunch the bleeding. The nurse rushed in and straightened her head and neck. She made a cold compress and used it on the affected areas.

'Did she bleed earlier?' the nurse asked. I answered that it had happened only now.

'It's not good if the bleeding starts. Her skull has been fractured in case you didn't know.' I felt a wave of anger course through me at that. Beinuo's eye was glazed over and she was unresisting as the nurse and I worked to stop the bleeding.

'Was it his work?' I had to ask the nurse. She nodded yes.

'It's a miracle she has survived this long. When she was brought in this afternoon, she looked so pale we thought she was already gone. We can't stop the bleeding. It'll be over soon.'

I hated the nurse for the emotionless manner in which she was discussing Beinuo's condition. But I knew that was the only way they could function; distancing themselves from the suffering and getting on with their jobs.

'Beinuo,' I called softly and held her hand. It was cold and unresponsive.

'Beinuo,' I called again.

'She's gone,' the nurse said behind me.

'No! No!' I cried but it was only too true. She was lying there motionless, beyond all pain. The nurse put a hand on my shoulder.

'Say your goodbyes. I will be outside. I'll clean her up when you are ready.'

Part Three

TWENTY

The Perfect Victim

'I'm going to the police to get him arrested!' I told Ato and Azuo when the funeral was over. I had already confronted him when he turned up at the hospital. 'You won't get away with this. You murdered her!' I had shouted when he came to take the body. He was quite angry at me and shook his fist in my face.

'Don't think you can threaten me and get away with it. My family is my property. I'll do what I like. You better keep out of our business or I'll make you regret it!' The nurses led me away and I tried to compose myself but I had already made up my mind to go to the police and have him convicted.

'They will ask you for proof,' Ato tried to reason with me, 'then what proof will you offer? The body has been disposed of and he will find witnesses to say she fell and hit her head on the concrete steps, fractured her skull and died. There is no point going to the police. He will make you look like a lunatic if you do that.'

Everything that Ato was saying was true. I would be asked for evidence and the only evidence I could come up with was my own suspicions and what I had seen of her injuries in the hospital and the dying confession of a very unhappy woman. Who would accept that as evidence?

I saw that the case was too flimsy to follow through. I could only pray that Uvi would be kept safe from her father. If I aggravated him any more he might not allow me to see her again. I had to be more cautious. Poor little Uvi clung to me throughout her mother's funeral. It was really too much for a child: she had lost her little brother a week ago and now her mother was dead too. I had no words to comfort her. I held her and held her and she fell asleep in my arms when she was too tired to cry. But when she woke up and remembered that her mother was gone, she wailed piteously and would not be comforted.

I waited for close to a week before visiting Uvi. She ran to me and put her head on my shoulder.

'Azuo Kevi, I'm so glad you've come.'

'I brought flowers, see? We can go and put them on your mother's grave.' I showed her the flowers and we walked hand in hand towards the grave. I removed faded wreaths and bouquets and put them to one side and placed my bouquet close to the headstone. We were not there long when the girl who worked in the house came running.

'Uvi, your father is calling you,' she said and tried to pull Uvi away from me. Uvi clung to me.

'I'll come by myself. I will, really.'

'He says you have to come now.' As they were struggling Meselhou came out and came striding towards us.

'You!' he lifted a finger and shouted at me, 'You! You're not to come back to this house. If you do, I will call the police and make a case against you. Do you hear?' I didn't say anything. Nor did I leave. I stood there and stared at him.

'Didn't you hear me? Uvi, let go of her hand now!' Uvi dropped my hand in fear.

'You will leave if you don't want to see me hurt her.' It was blackmail, and yet if I refused to go he was quite capable of hurting her just to spite me. I turned around and walked out of the gate.

'Beinuo is safe from that monster, but Uvi is still in danger,' I told Ato and Azuo.

'Kevi, she is his own daughter. What could he possibly do to her?' Azuo was trying to reassure me.

'I don't know, Azuo, I just feel that Uvi is not safe there.'

'The whole problem with Meselhou is that he is an only son,' Ato tried to explain. 'He's always had his way and it's possible that his parents spoiled him thoroughly as a child. You can see he is always ordering people around. That means he has never had to do anything for himself. His father dying early put him in a position of responsibility and power. As the only male, he got used to all the helpers obeying him and his mother always consulting him on the family business. He didn't want a wife who was more intelligent than him. Whoever was his wife had to be submissive and do his bidding. If she didn't listen to him, too bad for her. She would be beaten until she submitted.

Men like Meselhou have their own interpretation of our customary laws and act accordingly. You say he called Beinuo his property. But he was not right. If he mistreated her, her brothers would have the right to take her away from him. But she had no brothers or close male relatives. Men like that calculate their every move. Even if he is from a powerful family, he would not marry into another powerful family. He'd make sure that his wife comes from a lower income family as that makes her fearful of him and his higher status. Beinuo fitted into that role perfectly. She had no brothers; she had a stepmother who was only too happy to have her out of the house in the respectable role of a rich man's wife. He found a perfect victim!

Remember you said he pestered her to marry him and did not give up until she said yes? His type never take no for an answer. Anyone who says no to him is a challenge to his authority and his manhood. He will make your life miserable if you bring charges against him.'

'But what's wrong with our culture that it can allow this kind of behaviour? Why should we follow a culture that allows a man to be so cruel to his wife?' I asked angrily.

Azuo was in the kitchen where we were having this conversation. She put a hand on my shoulder.

'It's not the culture. It's the individual. You have to understand that, Kevinuo. You heard Ato say that her brothers had the cultural right to take a woman away from a cruel husband. Sad to say, Beinuo had no brothers. But in the absence of brothers, her male cousins could have stepped forward and taken her away. Even her father had every right to do that. But he did not. I suspect that Beinuo was too eager to run her own household that she entered into the marriage without carefully examining what kind of man he was. She might have displeased her father by the hasty nature of her marriage. Even without the option of sending Meselhou to prison her father could have brought a case against him by making an appeal to the elders. He didn't do that. Given that, it is not our place to do anything.'

It was very frustrating to conclude that the one man who could have protected Beinuo had chosen not to do anything. I had seen him at the funeral. He was weeping his eyes out. It must have been a mixture of remorse and frustration and self-condemnation. I hoped there was a lot of the last.

'I think we should find ways of reforming cultural practices so we can ensure justice for those who are truly in need of it. Meselhou threatened me, telling me to stay out of his family's business. There is something wrong about that. We always let it go when someone uses that argument. It's wrong. An outsider should be able to interfere and help when a child or a spouse is being abused and beaten within the family.'

'You have a good point there, Kevinuo,' Azuo agreed. 'Someone should bring that to the notice of the Village Council and let them make amendments to the customary laws. Meselhou should have been put behind bars. And Beinuo should have been given the help she needed to escape from that terrible man. And now it's too late.' Azuo placed her hands on my shoulders again. It was her way of letting me know she understood, that she cared.

But was it too late? Uvi was still there and if she was in danger, we should not allow another tragedy to happen.

TWENTY-ONE

Meselhou

All night I dreamed I was running away from Meselhou and a pack of dogs he had hired to hunt me. The dogs were there when I turned the corner and when I clambered up the slope, they snapped at my feet and ankles, trying to bite me. I desperately climbed, trying to get away from them, but when I got to the top, Meselhou was waiting for me with a gun pointed at my head. I let out a muffled scream, waking myself up. Luckily, I had not woken the others and I calmed down, relieved it was only a dream. Strange. Why would I dream that? Did that mean he intended to do me some harm? I had to be more careful now on, I thought, and got out of bed.

It was a work day so I got up and put the kettle on the gas stove. Azuo came downstairs and tried to get the fire going.

'I'll get that,' I told her as I arranged the kindling and burnt some paper and wood shavings. The kindling caught fire and I placed chopped wood on top.

'Always nice to have a fire in the morning,' Azuo commented. There was some frost on the windows reminding us that winter was still around. I remembered the stack of examination papers that were waiting for me. I would stay up late and get started on them, I promised myself.

Ato's day did not have to start as early as mine. His assistant opened the shop at 9 am and Ato would reach the shop half an hour later. For me, school started at 8.30 so my morning hours were rushed and stressful. I had no appetite in the mornings but forced myself to eat something before running out the door. It was the end of term before the school closed for the winter holidays. The headmaster wanted us to submit our papers within a week and have the students' mark sheets ready the following week. My class of sixty students was riotous when I entered the room. The whole morning went by in getting things for them to do. Now that exams were over, the students were frisky and not interested in any more academic work. At the end of the day I took a bundle of papers home with me. I would keep doing this the whole week. It just wasn't possible to concentrate in the noisy school compound.

Azuo had cooked a broth of dried meat and *kolar* beans and brown rice. It was winter food. She had added tomatoes and garlic paste to the broth and the aroma filled the whole kitchen. I went to my room to change and when I came back to the kitchen, Azuo ladled out food for me.

'I'm going to be a good girl today. I'm going to sit by the fire and correct answer scripts,' I said.

'Well, I can be your tea maker. I can make a cup of tea for every 20 answer scripts that you finish. Does that sound good?' We agreed it was a fair deal.

Ato came home late and ate alone while I worked on.

It had become quite dark when I decided to go to bed. I felt satisfied that I had cleared another bundle of papers, and still, I did not really feel peaceful. Work was a way of distracting my mind from its major preoccupation. How was Uvi? My thoughts turned in that direction as soon as I lay upon my bed. I imagined a scenario where I would take out all my savings, pack some clothing, and take her away with me to some place where no one would find us. And where would that be? What safe place could we go to? Perhaps to Shillong. I knew a Khasi girl named Belinda who had gone to school with us when her father was posted to Kohima in the Nagaland Secretariat. We became good friends and after she left Kohima we used to write to each other. Uvi and I could go to Shillong and ask Belinda to help us find a house for rent. I could say that Uvi was my daughter. If they asked about her father, I could say we were never married. I would be seen as one of the disrespectable women in society but it wouldn't matter so long as we could be safe from her father.

Eventually I would find work as a teacher in a school. I knew Shillong had many schools and I was sure I could teach in one or other of them. After all, I had a Bachelor's degree and had at least eight years of teaching experience behind me. Uvi could be admitted to the same school where I taught. She was soon turning five and would be ready for school. What better school than the one in which I worked so that we could both go to school together in the morning and eat our lunches in the teachers' room and go home together? Other students would hesitate to bully her knowing she was the teacher's daughter. And Uvi would make lots of new friends at school, she would learn to speak Khasi and, most importantly, in our new home she would be safe from anyone who wanted to harm her.

It was such a wonderful daydream that I was already shopping for her clothes in the Shillong stores, picking out the woollen checks that were so popular in Shillong, and taking them to the tailor to make little pinafores for her. I drifted off to sleep and slept soundly, waking up only when the neighbour's rooster had crowed several times.

It was a Friday. I tied up my papers and went off to school a few minutes earlier. On the way, I took a roundabout route that passed Uvi's house. There were a number of cars at the gate and several men milling about the house. I wondered what was going on but couldn't stop to find out. School was waiting and as a class teacher I didn't have the luxury of coming to work late. If I did that, my class would disturb the other classes and I would be called in by the Headmaster to explain why my class was left unattended in the first hour. When I reached school, I found that two of our teachers had taken leave on account of a death in their neighbourhood, and I missed out on my free period as I had to take one of their classes. I was so busy that I forgot all about the crowd I had seen outside Uvi's house in the morning.

At recess, I went straight to the teachers' room where we were served tea and biscuits. Sarah, one of my colleagues was chatting to another teacher and as I came in, she asked,

'I thought you would have gone to the funeral, Kevinuo?'

'I'm sorry, who died?' I asked a little uncertainly. It was Sarah's turn to look surprised.

'You were friends with his wife, I think. The husband died this morning. The name is Meselhou.'

The news was such a shock I had to sit down. I think I was gasping because Sarah quickly brought me a glass of water.

'Are you all right?' she asked with concern.

'I'm fine now. I didn't know anything when I passed their house this morning. I did notice there were a number of cars parked outside. Do you know how he died? Was he sick? I… I haven't been to their house recently.'

'I don't know how far this is true,' Sarah lowered her voice, 'but it appears that he and a friend were drunk and throwing stones at the CRP patrol at night. They were caught and beaten badly. I heard that Meselhou had a fractured skull when he was brought to hospital, but that it was already too late to save him. It's a terrible story. I don't know how much of it is true.'

I was slowly recovering from the shock of the news. Of course, it was a death. That explained the crowd of people in front of their house this morning. How silly of me not to realise something of that nature must have happened.

'What time is the funeral, do you know?' I asked.

'I heard Daniel say that it will be at 4 pm. He died a little before midnight so they won't keep the body for another night.' When people died in the night, it was the custom to observe a night-long vigil for the dead; relatives and neighbours would gather and sing hymns to keep the bereaved family company. That had already been taken care of last night and now preparations were going on for the funeral to be held in the afternoon. I took leave after recess, feeling a bit guilty as we were already two teachers short. At least I had taken their classes in the morning hours. I explained to the Headmaster that my best friend's husband had died. He said I should not have come at all and thanked me for helping in the morning. His considerateness made me feel better and I hurried home.

'Azuo, did you hear that Meselhou died last night?' Azuo was equally shocked.

'How dreadful! How did it happen? We never heard that he was sick.' I narrated all that I had heard and asked if she would come to the funeral. Azuo Zeü joined us wearing her black *lohe* and carrying her hymn book. I doubted that I would be doing much hymn singing but did not protest when Azuo thrust a hymnbook into my hand. I wanted to get there as soon as possible and see to Uvi.

There was a big crowd at the house. They made way for us as people always do at a funeral. When the new mourners come, the old mourners file out of the parlour and allow the newcomers the privilege of viewing the deceased. I noticed that Azuo and Azuo Zeü were praying when they reached the bed on which the body had been laid out but I felt dry-throated and dry-eyed. I had no tears. I stood and looked at the body. His skull was bandaged and his face was swollen on the left side. He was dressed in a suit and draped with a *lohe* from his chest downwards. Wreaths made of plastic flowers and bouquets of fresh flowers had been assembled in a corner of the room. I felt as though I was watching a movie; it was all so surreal. A week ago, this man had threatened me, and now he was lying lifeless before me. It was such a terrifying thought that I had to move away. I left Azuo and Azuo Zeü still standing by the coffin while I slipped into the next room to look for Uvi.

Young girls were milling about in the other rooms of the house, some of them serving tea to the mourners and the others just waiting around. I caught one of them who looked a little familiar and asked where Uvi was. She didn't know. She didn't even know who Uvi was. I looked for Beinuo's old room and found it locked. Where could Uvi be? Perhaps in her grandmother's room.

'Uvi!' I called softly as I continued to look for her. Where had she gone? When her mother died she had refused to leave her side. Now her father was dead and we couldn't find her. I instinctively went outside the house and walked towards Beinuo's grave. Uvi was standing there, alone, talking to her mother. I stopped and stood very still. I could not hear her words, but she was having an earnest conversation with her mother. When she paused, I coughed and she turned around, and ran to me. I saw she had been crying earlier but when she spoke to me, she controlled herself.

'I was telling Mother that Father is on his way to them now. He won't have reached yet because the pastor has to say the prayer to send him on his way.'

'That was very thoughtful of you,' I said and gave her my hand. Her brother's grave was beside Beinuo's. There was a wooden cross with a name on it. I couldn't read what was written on it.

'Do you know my brother's name?' she asked. I said no. She pulled me closer to the small grave and pointed at the wooden cross. *Keneizo James.*

'I call him Azo and he likes that.' I did not find it odd that Uvi was talking about her family members in the present tense. Perhaps that was her way of dealing with her many losses. By holding conversations with them as she was doing, she was bringing them back to life and back into her world and by doing that, perhaps she was able to cope with their absence. They were not gone, they were just somewhere else. And she could still reach them in this weird and rather wonderful way of hers.

'I hope you can talk to your father soon,' I said sincerely meaning every word.

'I'm sure I will. I'll have a lot of things to tell him,' she replied in all seriousness.

Meselhou's grave was not dug beside his wife's grave. It was on the other side of the garden where his father had been buried. I found that comforting.

TWENTY-TWO

Uvi

'It's not a ludicrous idea. I think it's an excellent idea,' Ato stated, 'who better to mother Uvi than you?' The three of us were sitting in the kitchen discussing the matter. Uvi was an orphan now. Her grandmother was getting on in years and Meselhou's sister had her own children to care for. Why not ask if I could bring up Uvi?

Azuo was more hesitant. *It is not culturally correct. We are not related by blood. No one has heard of such a thing.* She kept listing all the reasons why we should not broach the subject with the grandmother. I was so grateful that Ato was on my side. It might not be culturally correct but I felt we could reason with Meselhou's mother. She was not unreasonable. She would surely see the benefits of letting Uvi grow up in a household with a surrogate mother who could help her with her studies and give her the motherly affection that was taken from her so early in life.

'Who should go to talk to the grandmother?' Azuo asked doubtfully. 'I wouldn't know how to put such a thing across.'

'We'll all go,' I said. 'You, Azuo Zeü, Ato, and I. Ato and I will do the talking and you can affirm that it is an idea you fully support.'

'Isn't there an ancestor who could connect us to their family? Can you remember anyone, Azuo?' Ato quizzed her. Azuo wanted to know why he was asking that.

'It's easier to establish our cultural obligation as the reason for wanting to take Uvi in. If we could find one common ancestor, then I could present myself as a male relative with a responsibility to look after the orphaned child of my kinsman and they would find that harder to refuse.' Azuo smiled at Ato's audacity. But it set her thinking. Soon she said that she had to call Azuo Zeü over to help her remember. Between the two of them, they dug up not one but three ancestors that we shared with Meselhou's family. Now I was even more determined to go and talk to them.

To our amazement, Uvi's grandmother agreed to our request to take Uvi into our family and raise her as best we could. She said she had seen how much I cared for the child and how attached Uvi was to me.

'Please make time to bring her, now and then, to see her old grandmother. She is a good child. I am not able to give her what she needs. I am too old. Let me know if you need money at any stage.'

It was hard to believe but it was wonderfully true and Uvi came to live with us after two days. She was very happy. Every month we visited her grandmother and when we did that, she would go and talk to her mother and brother, bringing things to show them from her new house. Then she would cross to the other side of the garden and talk to her father.

We had our own routine, Uvi and I. Weekdays were working days when we got up early and got ready for school. It was always a bit of a struggle to get a sleepy five-year-old out of bed at 7 in the morning. She was very good at making up all kinds of excuses. Sometimes we played a game saying that the one who could jump out of bed first would get to eat two toffees after school. She loved toffees and would try really hard to beat me. Sometimes we both woke up late and then there would be no time for games and I just had to be firm with her and get her to cooperate. But Uvi had a sweet nature and I counted myself lucky to be her second mother.

In her first year of school she topped the class. She was so happy she came running to my room to show me her report card. The teacher had given her multiple stars. I lifted her up and swung her around.

'We are going to have a big party!' I promised her, and we did. Back in the house, Azuo cooked a chicken in country ginger and served it with steaming rice. Ato bought ice-cream for dessert and we were all very merry.

'If you keep doing this, we are all going to grow very fat,' Azuo Zeü teased her.

There are days when Uvi is a typical youngster, running in and out, climbing up chairs and falling and getting hurt and laughing at her own clumsiness. And there are some days when I find her standing at the window, looking out but gone quite inside of herself. I know she is growing too big to believe that her mother hears her when she talks to her at the grave. My heart feels too tight for my chest when I see that sadness on her little face. I feel powerless when that happens. I know it will always stay with her. It *is* her in a way, and it is what makes her so beautiful—that she chooses loving in spite of pain, that she chooses life in spite of loss.

Azuo and Azuo Zeü are getting on. Azuo is 60 and Azuo Zeü is 65. Atsa Nisoü lived to be 92 before she died peacefully in her sleep. She never became a Christian. Ato met a young woman who suited him and suited the rest of us. They have been married four years and have two children, a daughter and a son. They live in Apuotsa and Atsa Bonuo's old house which they renovated and gave a fresh coat of paint before moving in.

At school, Uvi is registered in her full name. *Melouvinuo.* The brave-hearted one. But everyone calls her Uvi. I know I can't go in and change everything for Uvi so that her past stops hurting her. I remember what Azuo said once long ago. I had asked her what life was about and she had replied with a smile, 'You live your best and your best is about doing the thing that gives others peace, because that is the very thing that will give you peace.' I have tried to put peace into Uvi's life and she returns that to me every day. There is always a risk that someday, when Uvi becomes a teenager, she might want to find the father she never knew. She might want to do that in ways I wouldn't recommend. But as I said, it is a risk. Love takes risks. If we give her the right kind of love, chances are she would be satisfied enough not to want to go looking for the other kind.

I am 35 years old now, a registered spinster. My chances at becoming a part of respectable society through marriage are very slim. Or are they? My rich, old widower has not showed up yet. We still have a little laugh about that, saying he will finally come hobbling with his walking stick apologising for the lateness.

Mapping Kohima

I am constantly curious about life in Kohima during certain periods of its history, in particular the periods before and after the Japanese invasion. Kohima in the period immediately following the Second World War sadly lacks documentation. The war came in and interrupted the narratives of our people quite abruptly. The writings of western anthropologists stopped in the early forties since the war made their stay tenuous. In spite of the colonial attitude applied to writing our cultures and the religious practices of our forefathers, one cannot be ungrateful for all the anthropological writing that exists on the Nagas from the nineteenth century right up to the war. But after the war there has been a big lacuna especially after the British Empire left India, taking its political officers with it. The book *Nagas in the 21st Century*, edited by Jelle J.P. Wouters and Michael Heneise, tries to close this lacuna. It is a first effort, an excellent one. I hope more will follow.

Kohima was established as the headquarters of the British in 1878. The decision was taken because the climate was more favourable, and it afforded a better command of the trade route on the road from Samagudting (Chumukedima) to Manipur. It was a decision taken by the offices of the Viceroy of India and the Governor General of India. On 12th November 1878, G.H. Damant, the Political Officer, took over office at the Kohima headquarters. He was soon after killed in the battle over Khonoma.

The present decade possibly offers the last opportunity to record the life of Kohima in the post-war years from its survivors' memories. Recreating pre-war Kohima using their memories was a challenging task but it was not impossible. My mother, Khrienguü Kire, could attest that the pillory set up by the British government was located at the former site of the yarn stores owned by Yachütuo and Zasitso at the end of the Mission road. It was used to deter drunkenness and brawling in public. Men caught stealing or brawling would be found in the pillory the next day as a demonstration of British justice.

According to T. Solo, his father Reverend Kumbho Angami had told him that the Kohima jail located below the North Police station was 'the only jail in those days of the late nineteenth and early twentieth centuries for criminals sentenced to death.' He recounted the case of one Lhousare of P. Khel Kohima who was convicted of setting fire to the houses in the village. Lhousare was sentenced to death and consequently hanged. In the book, *Heralding Hope*, J.B. Jasokie also recollects that the hanging of 'murderers and hard-core criminals' (p. 65) took place at the gallows in the police station. Corroborating my mother's information, T. Solo added that petty criminals 'were shackled in wooden frames and pilloried. This was publicly done in what is now the junction of Mission Compound and High School road on the eastern side of Vikrulie Belho's shop.'

Solo's decidedly visual description of the town follows:

'The centre of Kohima town was the traffic Police Point near the present Razhü Hotel where the Zero milestone stood on one side of the road, from where the measurement of all distances to other places from Kohima started. The town consisted of DC Court, and a few shops on the roadside in the centre of the town, Choto Bosti, Naga Bazaar, the Assam Rifles area, Chandmari, Dak Lane, the nearby Dhobi lane, and Mission Compound.'

The fledgling town of Kohima was originally centred around the present-day Naga Bazaar. Naga Bazaar was 'referred to as "Manipuri Market" because of the shops set up by persons from neighbouring Manipur' (*Heralding Hope*, p. 30) and was the only market at the time. It housed a tailoring shop, a grocery shop, a barber's shop, and a washerman lane, giving birth to the Hajam lane and Dhobi·lane. There was a guest house, Musafir Khana, with lodging facilities. Reportedly, the British administration concentrated its infrastructural facilities in this area.

To the south of Naga Bazaar, the Dak lane was established as a residential area for the *dak* runners who carried the post from Kohima to Mokokchung, Wokha, Henima, Tseminyu, and Jalukie. The *dak* was also transported by mule in some regions. Another important part of town appears to have been the Chotu Bosti, also known as Dobashi lane.

In the early days, there were a number of Marwari shops, of which one was known as Duosao's shop. The local people had given the trader the Angami name 'Duosao', and everyone referred to the shop as 'Duosao duka'. It was frequented by all the villagers. The Marwari shops sold all kinds of items such as thread, utensils, rice, matches, milk, and sugar. Other traders included men from the Jain community. One of them was given the Naga name 'Veso' by his local customers. Manipuri women sold eggs at the entrance to the Naga Bazaar.

1944 had been a long, hard year. People worked hard to get their lives back on course. When some semblance of normalcy was restored, a few educated men were very concerned for the younger people who were missing out on schooling. These men were Neiliehu Belho and Vibeilie Belho who had passed High School. Men from Kohima village helped them to set up makeshift sheds to be used as a school while the school buildings were being repaired. The school begun by Neiliehu and Vibeilie ran for some months.

However, the government closed down this privately-run school and appointed a teacher to reopen the Mission School. Mr Lhuviniu Lungalang was appointed to look after the school with the help of the other local teachers. The new teachers, Rosalind, Putsüre and Lucy Dino Phewhuo, Esther, Pelhoutuoü, and Vibeilie taught alongside older teachers like Rüzhükhrie, Shürholhoulie, Duosielhou, and Pfeno.

After several months, Reverend Supplee came back to Kohima with his family. On his return, Supplee shifted the school into the abandoned hospital premises. The Mission School was a government school. In 1941, the Mission School was upgraded to Class 10. After functioning at the abandoned hospital buildings for some years, the school shifted once more in 1950 to its present location in the area that has now come to be known as High School colony. Janikhoü Savino affirms that the school was extended to Class 10 with the help of the parents of the students. Hers was the first batch to appear for the matriculation exam in the Mission School. She also adds that horse-drawn carts plied on the roads in the pre-war days. Certainly, horses were used as a means of transport by the officials in the government. There were otherwise only two cars in the town, the first belonging to the District Commissioner and the other, to the missionary Supplee.

The buildings used as hostels by the Mission School students were completely destroyed during the war. Reopening school was one of the major efforts at restoring normalcy to the town. Whilst repairs were going on, the Mathematics teacher, Rüzhükhrie, often took his students to his house and gave them lessons rather than waste a day of teaching.

Education became a priority after the war. Before the war, around 1936, a businessman named John Angami started a school in the Viswema village area so that students in the southern villages did not have to travel as far as Kohima to get education. It was called the John Institute, and DC Pawsey donated tin sheets for the school buildings, and the rest of the building materials for the school were given by John Angami. After the war, DC Pawsey encouraged its development into a High School. Besides students from the villages of Viswema, Khuzama, Jakhama, and Kigwema, the school also attracted students to the south of Viswema such as Mao and its neighbouring regions.

My mother and other survivors remember the pre-war hospital as a small one located in the heart of the town. It was begun as a ten-bedded dispensary which was upgraded to a civil hospital in the present location of the Union Baptist Church and the former Kohima College building. It was extensively damaged during the war. For a short period after the war, the hospital was located at the Mission Compound in makeshift buildings with tin roofs (T. Solo). Work on the hospital would begin the following years at Serzou.

According to R. Kevichüsa, Lord Wavell had asked Pawsey what could be done for the Nagas in recognition of their services rendered to the British during the war. Pawsey's reply was, 'A good, modern hospital.' Pawsey travelled to Delhi and asked the government for the funds and the hospital was named the Naga Hospital. Construction work on the hospital began in 1946 and was more or less completed in 1949. Bulldozers were employed to widen the site. R. Kevichüsa adds that the hospital was a gift to the Naga people (*Heralding Hope*, p. 41).

The Naga hospital area is called Serzou. As a matter of fact, Serzou is a large area starting from the perennial water source (below the box-cutting, leading down from the upper road to connect with the main highway) and continuing till the location of the hospital. At the hospital site, several buildings were constructed to accommodate the different departments that would provide maternity services and basic medical services to the public.

Oral sources on post-war Kohima give general pictures of the massive work of rebuilding that took place when the war was over. DC Pawsey had directed all administrative efforts into helping the native population to rebuild their homes and lives. The DC and his men registered the amount of damage each household had suffered and they paid compensation according to the information rendered. The government arranged this compensation under the Assam Relief Measures scheme. It included distribution of rations such as rice, tea, sugar, and salt to the local population. The rations were distributed over a long period of time until the civilian population could fend for themselves again.

After the war, the government worked very hard to restore normalcy in the affected areas. It was a full-time job to provide shelter for those who had lost their homes. Tin and timber were provided in addition to sums of money for the work of rebuilding. The pre-war houses were built of bamboo and wood with thatch roofing. After the war, all the newly constructed houses had corrugated iron roofing. The reconstruction work in Kohima village and town was completed around early 1945.

Post-war Kohima saw immense changes as the society made a huge transition from a largely rural and village-based agricultural society to a modernised, town-based, semi-urban community. For the first time, Nagas took to trading on a much more professional scale than their forefathers. Neilasa Kesiezie set up a hardware store. He was the first Naga entrepreneur in Kohima town. Besides Neilasa, others who opened shops were Zasitso, Duo-o, Kevirüya, Suosahie, Yachütuo, and the men who ran the NCS, the Naga Cooperative Services. Pawsey encouraged and supported Nagas who wanted to try their hand at trading. The NCS sold sugar, tea, and other grocery items and it was also licensed to sell petrol and kerosene, which it did for a period of time.

After the war, Pawsey summoned A. Kevichüsa to his office.

'You can ask for land or any property from the British government,' he told Kevichüsa. Pawsey meant that it would be by way of rewarding him for his services during the war. Kevichüsa did not ask for land for himself, but he asked for land for the Naga Cooperative Society, which was granted. This information was rendered by Metsiü Iralu and Meneü Kevichüsa about their late father.

I am including the information provided by people born and bred in Kohima town in the fifties. By the beginning of the fifties, Kohima seems to have rapidly become a small yet vibrant centre of trade for the surrounding villages. Atuo Mezhür recollects that he used to walk from the war cemetery to town every morning in the mid-fifties. 'I remember seeing shops such as Doss & Co., Chakravorty, and the T. Khel store. The house where Neilasa and Zasitso hardware stores are presently located was formerly a Manipuri hotel. It was the property of the NCS. The T. Khel store was owned by some members of the Solo clan. They also sold hardware as at that time people were rebuilding their lives after the war had ended. Many Manipuris had hardware shops. They must have been there from the forties.'

The Kohima Pharmacy, the first and the oldest pharmacy in town, was established in the year 1953. Besides medicines, the proprietor Dr Neilhouzhü Kire also sold footballs, an amusing fact, because he loved the game. Jadial Sekhose was one of the first bakers in Kohima. He was trained by British cooks and ran a home-based bakery producing cakes and bread. In a 2004 interview in *Heralding Hope*, Ashim Roy mentioned opening the Kohima bakery in 1951–52 with his wife Kelakieü along the Mission road. The bakery sold cookies, bread, and round salted biscuits. The Jadial bakery is still in business to this day while the Kohima bakery was converted into a pharmacy.

Tin houses constructed along the Mission road were eagerly turned into shops by local traders. In 1958, Benjamin Sekhose opened the first book store called the Peak Agency Book Store. Benjamin was a teacher in the Government High School at the time. He was concerned that students were suffering because they could not get textbooks. He began to order and sell textbooks, Bibles, hymnbooks, calendars, stationery, and Christian literature. Peak Agency was housed in a wooden building which has since burnt down. The original location of Peak Agency was adjacent to Meyase Hotel. Visier Sanyü recollects that, in the sixties, his brother Perhicha shared a shop with two other traders, one of whom was a Sema lady running a tailoring business. Further up the road was one of the first shoe stores opened by Munshi, a Kashmiri gentleman who was married to an Angami lady.

Along the line of shops toward the police point, Tilok Thapa opened what could have been Kohima's first hosiery store. He later changed it to a cloth store with the name 'T.B. Thapa and Sons'. Eventually he opened a popular tailoring store named Student Tailoring Shop which was located in the same premises as the cloth store.

In the days before prohibition, there were liquor stores in town selling spirits. It was in the sixties that Leo Angami opened a licensed liquor store opposite Razhu Hotel. There was another liquor store near the present Viliethie Complex. All these liquor stores were closed after the Prohibition Act came into place and the shops moved on from selling liquor to selling automobile parts.

The first church in Kohima was called the Kohima Baptist Church. According to information supplied by Pastor Sehu Belho, it was the oldest church in Kohima. The first church was established by Reverend C.D. King without any native converts on 29 March 1883. Lhousietsü Rutsa became the first convert from the village and was baptised on 21 June 1885. However, he gave up his new faith and returned to the old religion. Sieliezhü Sorhie of Kohima village was the next person to be converted. Sieliezhü was baptised on 30 August 1885. During a period, he returned to the old religion, but was restored once again to the church. The name of the church was changed to Kewhira Kehou and Sieliezhü became the first pastor. Until the year 1922, the Kewhira Kehou worshipped in the Mission Chapel, but due to the upgradation and expansion of the Mission School, the church shifted location. It was a woman named Visaü, the mother of Reverend Kruneizhü Ciesotsü who gave her land to the church in the Tsieramia area of Kohima village. Pastor Sehu Belho, affirms that the name of the native church found in church records is 'Kewhira Kehou.'

During the war, the church building was destroyed and had to be rebuilt. In the middle of the 1970s, the church was moved to its present site near D-Khel as a major landslide had affected the church lands and graveyard. The graves were exhumed and shifted to the new church graveyard near Don Bosco. The same landslide in 1974 took away the colony below the graveyard where my grandfather's house and his friend Reverend Kumbho's house were located. It swept all the way down, affecting the areas below the Mission road where hostel buildings and Dino Phewhuo's house used to stand.

Kohima is home to people of different religions. The Sikh Gurdwara at D-Block was begun in 1942. It used to cater 'to 100 or more members—consisting of local residents, government officials and army personnel—and the feeding of devotees at the *langar* on every Sunday, used to be an immensely popular event for the neighbourhood children' (*Heralding Hope*, p. 34). Today, the gurudwara is looked after by 'a Sikh carpenter who works part time as priest. He said there are only six families left in Kohima' (David Kire).

The one mosque in the town 'was built by early Muslim settlers (led by one Hafiz Abdul Jaleel from Manipur) in the late nineteenth century' in the year 1885 (*Heralding Hope*, p. 34).

The Digambar Jain temple was built in 1920 and is one of the oldest buildings in Kohima. Hiralal Sethi was the first Jain to become a carriage contractor for the British in 1888. He was soon joined by other Jain families and they eventually constructed the S.D. Jain temple at Keziekie, North Block on land given to them by the British government (*Heralding Hope*, p. 33).

As the population of Kohima continued to grow, socially concerned individuals saw the demand for education and they worked on opening more schools. The Kohima English School was established in 1958 by Samuel Mezhür. In 1959, Reverend Beilieü Shüya became the headmistress of the newly opened Baptist English School. In an interview, she said that she wanted to help those parents who desired to give a good education to their children. She observed that people's priorities had changed in the post-war generation, and she saw the need for more local teachers, which could only be fulfilled by creating more schools and providing education in remote areas. With this focus in mind she opened the National School in 1964. After this effort, she opened two more private schools, one in Phek and one in Pughoboto. Both these schools were absorbed by the government schools in the two places.

Meanwhile, Rano Shaiza started a private school called Children's Christian School in 1967. According to her son Aziebu Shaiza, the school was recognised in 1972. Rano Shaiza's eldest daughter Vitsomeno Shaiza recounts that her parents initially started a shop called Gill Garments which was located in Dr Setu's town house that they had rented. The shop sold wool sweaters and ladies' garments brought all the way from Ludhiana Mills. This was in the late fifties and early sixties.

'The first shop was burnt down by either the Assam Police or the Armed Forces. The second house that was constructed had ceilings made from the empty plywood tea chests that my father, Lungshim Shaiza, had collected from the shops Doss & Co. and Chakravorty. Gill Garments later on shifted to its new premises at High School road in a rented house that was the property of Dr Neilhouzhü Kire,' Vitsomeno added. Lungshim Shaiza was the first car owner to drive a vintage car on the streets of Kohima in the sixties. The family ventured into supplying school uniforms and the Chari Departmental Stores was opened a decade later.

A major part of social change in the sixties was the

transition from kerosene lamps to electric bulbs. Villages to the south of Kohima have an interesting history of generating electricity. Amongst these, Viswema took the lead having already established one of the first private schools, the John Institute. In a joint effort, the villages were able to generate electricity from the Keho river. They used a makeshift micro hydroelectric plant which was put together from scraps of metal, most of it abandoned war materials. The project took off under the supervision of a Manipuri technician.

Former Electrical Engineer Lanu Toy recalls that 'it was at a time when the only electricity that was available in the Naga Hills was in the form of batteries and small generators for operating message transmitting equipment and for electrifying the residence of the Deputy Commissioner of Kohima and the SDO of Mokokchung. It was only in 1961 that electricity was made available in Kohima basically for administrative needs, through small diesel engine generating plants.' When Mr Lanu Toy took over as Head of the Electricity Department in 1966, only five administrative towns had electricity in a limited scale using diesel generating units. He arranged to purchase bulk power from Assam and started constructing high tension transmission lines to reach not only the administrative towns but interior villages as well. Mr Toy has put on record that the cooperation and support from the villagers was exemplary.

The landscape of Kohima has changed over the years, which is only to be expected. Part of the change in the landscape includes the transformation of public recreation spaces into commercial spaces. Phoolbari was a small park with a fountain and a flower garden formerly located at the present Tibetan Market complex a few metres from the Oking hospital. It has had to give way to the incursion of a growing urban community.

Spirit Sightings

In the book there are references to spirit sightings by Ania Nisoü. The Angamis were familiar with spirit sightings, and as recorded, such sightings continued after the Second World War was concluded in the Naga Hills. One of my narrators, Marion Sircar, attests that she and her cousin, Aleü Bara, both aged around six years, often saw a spirit couple perched on the top of a bent bamboo. The couple would be dressed in different costumes on different days. Marion and another cousin saw a spirit on the hill slope opposite their house which corresponds to the spirit Keshüdi that Ania Nisoü was familiar with. It was a full moon night and the spirit came towards them aggressively. She recalls that it was very big, and its size alerted them to the fact that it was a spirit.

My grandfather was returning late one evening when he saw a man coming up the path carrying a winnowing mat. As the man drew closer, the winnowing mat grew higher and higher and the man carrying it also increased in size. With a shock, Grandfather realised it was a spirit and he threw his lantern at it as he jumped into the neighbouring compound.

People claim that spirits have favourite haunts such as village ponds, the village gate, big boulders, great trees, abandoned houses and gullies, and graveyards. After the war, the new spirits that were sighted were the spirits of the soldiers who died in the war.

There are not many houses from the forties and fifties that have survived the onslaught of increase in population and modernisation. The Mission Chapel survived the war, but it did not survive the zeal of the modernists. The little mahogany house is still serving its purpose and has faithfully housed the offices of the Baptist College. T. Solo affirmed that it is the oldest building in Kohima and was built in 1914. None of the mission buildings was destroyed during the war. However, the first Mission house which had been built by Clark, was badly damaged so it was dismantled after the war. It was a small house designed like a Naga house. Reverend Supplee constructed the present Mission House on his return from America. One of the houses destroyed in the neighbourhood was A. Kevichüsa's house. It was built by his father, Nisier Angami, and was destroyed in 1944. The present family house being used as Razhü Pru Hotel was built in 1946–47 by Kevichüsa (T. Solo).

Kohima town has developed exceedingly from the little plainsman's village, Tephriera, as it was originally called, into its present-day city proportions. The population is mixed and spills over so that the original boundaries between Kohima and its neighbouring villages in the south and north are almost becoming blurred. Many forest areas have given way to private residences. Azuo Zeü and her sister Khonuo would have a lot of trouble recognizing places and even registering that this was once their hometown. Hopefully there will be some wise children in Uvi's generation who will see to it that the legacy upon which their civilisation has been built is not completely wiped out.

The Political Background

The Naga Hills were under British occupation from 1832 to 1947. It was a period where the British saw great resistance to the occupation from the Naga tribes. Several expeditions were made against 'rebel villages' to bring them into submission to British rule. The last battle of Naga resistance was fought by the village of Khonoma in 1879. The battle ended with the enactment of a treaty between the two forces.

During the First World War, about 2,000 Nagas were recruited as labour corps and sent to France. The Naga tribes experienced a deep sense of unity and it is believed that on their return they formed the Naga Club in 1918, an organisation designed to protect the socio-political identity of the Naga tribes. T. Solo has however argued otherwise in his article, 'Story of Naga Club and Simon Commission' (*Nagaland Post*, 24 June 2017) and writes that the Naga Club was actually conceived as a club for the native government servants. Before the war, the present Ozone Café building was the site of the European club, an exclusive institution providing entertainment and leisure activities for European officers posted to the Headquarters. 'Non-whites, Indians or the Nagas were not ever allowed into the white Club. It was exclusively for the Europeans. The native government servants took the cue to form a similar native body.' Its development into a politically conscious institution would only be a natural progression, keeping in mind the changes happening within the British South Asian empire in that period.

When the Nagas became aware that the British would soon depart from their South Asian empire, a memorandum was submitted by the Naga Club to the Simon Commission in 1929. It stated that the Nagas should be excluded from the coming political reforms, underlining that the Nagas—who were neither Hindu nor Muslim—did not wish to be part of the Indian Union.

Acting on the Simon Commission, the Government of India Act was passed in 1935 stating that the Naga Hills District was to be treated as an 'Excluded Area' and any Act of the Federal Legislature or Assam Legislature would not apply to it. The Naga Hills District Council was formed at the initiative of DC Pawsey. It was converted into the Naga National Council in 1946. The NNC declared that it stood for the solidarity of the Naga tribes.

In 1947, Sir Akbar Hydari, Governor of Assam, made a Nine-point Agreement with the Naga leaders providing legislative, judicial and executive powers as well as protection of lands and resources. In Naga history, it was known as 'The Hydari Commission,' but there was disagreement over the interpretation of the ninth clause of the agreement, and subsequently it was not implemented. Indian independence was declared on the 15th August 1947 and the Naga Areas continued to be regarded by the Indian government as part of the District of Assam.

A plebiscite was conducted in 1951 showing that 99 per cent of the population had voted for Naga sovereignty, the results of which were sent to the Prime Minister of India, but this was ignored by the government. The first Indian General Elections in 1952 were boycotted in the Naga Hills.

In 1953, the Assam Maintenance of Public Order Act was passed. The Act sanctioned arrests without warrants, imposed collective fines and outlawed public speeches and meetings. The Naga Hills Disturbed Area Ordinance and Assam Public Order Maintenance Act were enforced in 1956. In March 1956, the NNC formed the Federal Government of Nagaland.

The Armed Forces Special Powers Act was passed in 1958. It sanctioned search and seize without warrant and shooting to the causing of death, with complete protection of the military and paramilitary forces from legal charges.

Each of the three Acts restricted movement of the civilian population and legalised the torture and arrest of villagers on the charge that they were helping the Naga Underground members. Villages were subjected to grouping, prevented from going to the fields, and women were raped by the armed forces in several incidents. Burning of villages and burning of granaries were some of the tactics employed to wipe out the Naga freedom movement.

In 1963, the state of Nagaland was inaugurated, followed by the cease-fire agreement of 1964. Later on, both groups accused each other of abrogating the terms of the cease-fire.

In 1975, the Shillong Accord signed by the representatives of the underground organisations and the Indian Government stated that the Nagas would accept the Indian Constitution. The Accord was considered as signed under duress and, therefore, its legality came into question. Nevertheless, it created factionalism and infighting among the Naga groups.

The National Socialist Council of Nagaland was formed in 1980, followed by the breakaway of the NSCN (K) in April 1988 led by S.S. Khaplang.

The long history of brutal military occupation has been traced as one of the major factors behind feelings of emasculation and frustration experienced by a section of males in Nagaland. Prohibition has simply made the problem more complex by its circumstantial creation of the smuggling racket in alcohol. The nexus between politics and alcohol abuse and an underworld that thrives on the existence of prohibition and political instability became an unfortunate reality.

The Nagaland Liquor Total Prohibition Act 1989

The Nagaland Liquor Total Prohibition Act of 1989 states that it is 'an Act to totally prohibit possession, sale consumption, and manufacture of liquor in and of import and export thereof in the State of Nagaland.'

The Act 'received the assent of the Governor of Nagaland on 13 April 1990 and was published in the *Nagaland Gazette Extraordinary* dated 24 April 1990.'

It sets out that there will be total prohibition of liquor, making Nagaland a dry state. No person would be allowed to

(1) Transport, import or possess liquor,
(2) Sell or buy liquor,
(3) Consume liquor,
(4) Manufacture liquor, and
(5) Use or keep any material, utensil, implement or apparatus whatsoever for manufacture of liquor.

It added that from the commencement of this Act:

(1) Nagaland shall be a dry state, and
(2) There shall be total prohibition of liquor in the state.

The Act clarified that certain parties such as Armed Forces personnel, deads of foreign countries, ambassadors, envoys, honorary counsels, or trade and commerce representatives of a foreign country would be exempted from the prohibition, along with persons using alcohol for bonafide medicinal, scientific and industrial purposes. The Prohibition Act is very lengthy, consisting of 85 points altogether.

Smuggling alcohol takes place on the state borders of Assam and Nagaland. The statistics for alcohol related deaths are not available. Adulterated alcohol has been analysed as containing methanol, and other toxins including kerosene. Alcoholism is still a major social problem and the solution presented by the church—prohibition—has not solved it. On the other hand, deaths from adulterated alcohol continue unabated, and there is no effective mechanism to control the flow of adulterated alcohol into the state.

Glossary of Angami Words

Azuo	Mother
Apuo	Father
Atsa	Grandmother
Apuotsa	Grandfather
Ami	maternal uncle

The use of the pronoun 'n': When the speaker is talking to a younger person the polite way is to use the kinship terms by including the pronoun 'n' which means 'your.' Thus, 'nzuo' means your mother, 'npuo', your father, 'ntsa', your grandmother, 'npuotsa', your grandfather, and 'nmi' means your uncle.

Gazie	edible herb belonging to the nettle family
Terhuomia	the spirits
Genna-day	a *genna*-day is a non-work day when it is taboo to do certain kinds of labour.

Genna-days are observed in the old religion to prevent damage to crops by natural calamities.

Keshüdi   native name of a fearsome spirit, usually gargantuan in size

Lohe   black body-cloth with red and green stripes on the border

Lora Mhoushü   white woman's body-cloth and waist-cloth with geometrical patterns